Rural Sports Library

GEORGE DOGGET
GAME-KEEPER

2

GEORGE DOGGETT
GAME-KEEPER

A Tale of Devon

Dr. P H Mules

Beech Publishing House
Station Yard
Elsted Marsh
MIDHURST
West Sussex GU29 0JT

© BPH Ltd , 2009

ISBN 1-85736-266-4
SECOND Edition 2004
THIRD Edition 2009

A Classic Tale

**British Library Cataloguing-in-Publication
Data**
A catalogue record for this book is available
from the British Library.

Beech Publishing House
**Station Yard
Elsted Marsh
MIDHURST
West Sussex GU29 0JT**

CONTENTS

This is a classical story of life long ago when the Squire was the principal figure in a location. He would be surrounded by Gamekeepers and other staff. There would also be the occupants of the village and the essential personnel, such as the doctor and vicar. They took their places and existed together, all concerned with the activities of the area.

In effect, the tale represents a part of our social history and therefore makes fascinating reading. More so, when told with the skills of Dr Mules, MD, whose writing can be likened to Thomas Hardy and other leading writers who recorded the lives of our ancestors in a warm and sympathetic way.

The period covered did not prohibit the shooting of any wild birds, but many are now protected. But in any case the Squire and George Doggett would follow the rules of conservation, thus protecting any rare species.

Many new illustrations have been found to augment those in the first edition. In them selves they tell a story and are of great interest.

Joseph Batty   **Elsted Marsh**

6

1
GEORGE DOGGETT
GAMEKEEPER
INTRODUCTION

THE MANOR HOUSE

8

CHAPTER I.

GEORGE DOGGETT, HIS **X**.

" DANG 'em, dang 'em. I'll be even wi 'em yet." It was in November, just in the gloaming-, that George Doggett uttered these words.

For nearly a century had the Doggetts, from father to son, lived and watched amongst the Westcombe Woods, and if the velveteen coat, and neat leather continuations did symbolise their office, they were proud of the badge, and felt that earth held no more desirable heritage thanthat of " Keepers of Westcombe." Of Westcombe itself it is hard to say enough.

Situate on the borders of Devon and Somerset, yet nestling amongst the coombes of Devon—the Pearl West—its lovely woods, rich in variety and growth, clothe the hills and valleys in a dress of vivid green or russet brown, as Spring gives way to Autumn, or Autumn is in turn displaced by Spring.

George Doggett -- Gamekeeper

Nature has indeed been lavish, for here in the beautiful valley of the Axe has she perfected her handiwork, by winding a silver thread, in and out, through vale and mead, until the eye, unable longer to follow its tortuous course, catches it as glistening points until it is finally lost to view.

The Keepers of Westcombe

Well may the "Keepers of Westcombe" be satisfied with their lot, for their lines have fallen in pleasant places, and the name of Doggett is held in respect and honour; for not only does the Squire repose implicit faith in their honesty, but he looks upon them as part and parcel, of the estate ; so that in his eyes it is as essential for the well- being of Westcombe that a "Doggett" shall rule at the lodge, as that a " Wynheard "* shall reign at the hall.

How was it then that the equanimity of the ruling Doggett was disturbed sufficiently to account for the " grip of the gun, and look on the face," so suggestive of volcanic conditions .   For some time the keeper had feared that his pheasants were being spirited, away ; in other words, " poached ;" and as he listened, his trained ear detected such a notable decrease in the rising of the birds for their nightly roost.

Towards the West—its lovely woods, rich in variety and growth, clothe the hills and valleys in a dress

---

* **Pronounced " Winyard."**

The Gamekeepers

in a dress of vivid green or a russet brown, as Spring gives way to Autumn, or Autumn is in turn displaced by Spring, that doubt became a certainty, and certainty produced the remarks which head this chapter. Nor was this all, for his mental perturbation was so obvious, that Shot—the black retriever—looking up in his master's face with boundless sympathy in his beautiful brown eyes, forgot to wag his tail.

The Black Retrievers

Curse of the Poachers

That poachers should venture on the estate at all was as gall and wormwood to honest George, for born and bred amongst the the villagers, he had always cultivated friendly relations with them; but for their unlawful depredations to take place in the **Holmwood** -- of the special cover, the very apple of the Squire's eye—was a sin of such enormity, that George Doggett again breathed vengeance not loud, but deep, and turning on his heel, slowly walked away, cogitating how he might defeat these, his natural enemies, and "cast them in their own net." Who was it? Slowly mentally revolving the antecedents of different ne'er-do-wells, he ruminated thus—

> *"Taint Sam Byles—'s wife won't let un—*
> *an' Joe Targut's keeping close zince*
> *I drashed un zo, last vall."*

A gleam, distinct, though transient, broke through the gloom of his countenance as he remembered the prompt but salutary lesson scored on the back of the erring Joseph Pike! and here the keeper's thoughts rested for a time. Was it Pike ? He seemed likely; but as an experienced detective knows by the mark of the tool what cracksman has been at work, so after weighing the pros and cons, " Pike" was rejected; and the keeper, again a fault, lost himself in vain conjecture.

13

PHEASANTS COCK & TWO HENS

Pheasants -- these became
the target for poachers

As he slowly walked home, unmindful of all save the bitterness of impotence, he was roused from his unpleasant reflections by the sight of the under-keeper, Joe Butt, preparing the dogs' supper. The matter was so serious and pressing, that without loss of time Joe was made acquainted with the keeper's suspicions. Now Joe was known to be sententious, a man of few words, but into those words he managed to compress a good deal of significance. So, when the fact was announced,

"There's a many veasants missin' there were suggestions.

" Sam Byles ?" suggested the keeper. "'Es missus," said Joe, with a shake of the head which added volumes, and tallied so exactly with Doggett's own view that "Joe Targut" was propounded at once. " A' dussn't, 's afeard o' a lickin," replied Joe.

The ground thus cleared, Pike was ventured; and here Joe found it necessary not only to scratch his head, but to gaze over the tops of the trees and cast a circumferential glance around before replying, "a' couldn't do ut," and having no one to propose on his own account, left with the cheering announcement, "pup's got distemper."

George Doggett -- Gamekeeper

2

THE
NIGHT WATCH

THE SEARCH WAS ON

18

CHAPTER II.

THE NIGHT-WATCH.

A PIPE and good night's rest brought Doggett into a less disconsolate frame of mind. The pheasants had gone, and could not be recovered; to save the remainder, as well as catch the culprits, was now the question. That the Holmwood would be again attacked was more than probable, therefore their plans were laid accordingly and as there was a full moon that night, and probabilities were in favour of another attempt.

Setting Up A Watch

Joe Butt, with two watchers retained for special service, set out at ten o'clock for the keeper's lodge. The night was perfect of its kind, for a sharp frost had already sprinkled the woodland paths with diamonds glittering from a thousand points, as they crunched and crackled under foot; the shadows cast by the waving branches were distorted and ghost-like, and the weird sounds of the soughing and wailing wind rose and fell upon the listening ear. As neither Joe Butt nor his companions were in an appreciative mood for the beautiful in nature, their feelings may be fairly represented by the remark of one of the watchers, who observed, " I do wish they poarchers were drownded, I do, an' I wor' at Blue Cow."

Joe Butt responded with a sympathetic grunt, for it was no secret that the tap-room of the Blue Cow took a heavy toll of Joe Butt's weekly wage.

The other watcher, to beguile the tedium of the way, burst forth into song, which, rousing all the dogs round the village, produced such an emphatic " Zhut up, can't 'ee," from Joe Butt, that in silence they gained Doggett's door.

" Now, Joe, have a drop o' zumatt to keep cold out, and let's be off," was Doggett's greeting. Joe responded by solemnly draining his portion, wiping the mug with his sleeve, and handing it to his neighbour, who followed Joe's lead in its entirety, and handed the mug, much lightened, to watcher No. 2. Then, shouldering their cudgels, they sallied forth.

" What shall 'e do wi 'cm, Joe, ef zo be 'e do catch 'em ? " said a watcher. " Drash 'em, an' take 'em to Zquire," replied Joe.

" I d' warnt Joe'll drash 'em fast enurf, ef 'e do catch 'em," said the other watcher, ministering to Joe's vanity in the present, and anticipatory of favours to come. Further conversation was checked by the deposit of watcher No. I at his post, after parting instructions from Doggett to run to his whistle, or to shout if he saw aught of a poacher. In due course the second watcher was placed ; thirdly Joe; lastly Doggett, who, ensconcing himself behind a bank in the driest hollow he could find, prepared for coming events.

It may be that many of my readers have never spent a night watch ; those that have spent a night in watching, know the strain of sitting hour after hour, waiting for that which may never come. Joe Butt felt it, and at last, to relieve his cramped and weary limbs, as well as break the monotony of his vigil, stole slowly, and as he hoped, silently along. The moon was at the full, but occasional passing cloudlets obscured her brightness; with each returning gleam came those weird shadows so deceptive and startling, and Joe, as he stopped from time to time with a nervous sharpening of all his senses, fancying he heard stealthy footsteps moving towards him, grasped his cudgel, and awaited further developments.

A Poacher is Spotted

At this critical moment a cloud of unusual density passed over the moon, and in the darkness Joe was only dimly conscious of the figure of a man creeping gently forward. To hesitate was to lose this golden opportunity of covering him, Joe Butt, with honour and glory. With a shout to warn Doggett and the watchers, he sprang out, single handed, to encounter the enemy, and applied his cudgel with such emphasis that had it fallen on the intruder's head, as Joe intended, this history would never have been written.

Warned by Joe's shout, his blows were met by a vigorous counter stroke, and at it they went, no quarter being given or expected. Three or four minutes elapsed, during which nothing but the blows and hard breathing of the two men could be heard, except an occasional ejaculation from the luckless Joe, who was getting sadly the worst of the encounter. By this time the watchers had come up, and were encouraging one of the two men whom they took for the keeper, with cries of " Well done, Jarge, gi ut un, cure un o' poarching this time."

Poachers Face-to-Face

But as the darkness prevented them from separating keeper from poacher, they could only dodge around waiting for the reappearance of the light. At last it came, revealing Joe in a very battered condition, but full of fight; and Doggett, his unsuspected adversary, scarcely much better. The two men, dropping their sticks, gazed blankly at each other, whilst the watchers, unable to comprehend the state of affairs, awaited explanations.

It was a Moon-lit Night

Doggett first found his tongue with, "Wy, dang it all, Joe, be that thee?" "Ay," replied Joe, "tis I, zure to the company generally, "I made zartin zure 'e wor a poarcher." Mutual explanations followed, and amid some merriment, in which Joe, with his ' fingers often wandering to his scalp, did not join, Doggett to see the Squire in the morning.

3
AT THE
SIGN OF
THE BLUE COW

The Blue Cow Inn

CHAPTER III
AT THE SIGN OF THE BLUE COW

VERY WELL KNOWN was the Blue Cow, an unpretentious hostelry of the usual village type of which various landlords had been old servants at the Hall. Over the door in bold letters , all men were informed that there was "excellent accommodation for man and beast"— interchangeable terms I regret to say occasionally—and that one Thomas Trout was "licensed to sell cider, beer, wine, and spirits, to be drunk on the premises," a permission which a few of the choice spirits of Westcombe interpreted literally, to the scandal of the Vicar, who preached against drunkenness twice every year.

But there were others who took only their modest stoup, and except under circumstances so exceptional that we may dismiss them from our minds, went home at regular hours, and in a regular manner.

A Village Character

Foremost amongst these, the Father of this simple Senate, was old William Mitchell, a typical West Country husbandman, always dressed in the same sort of smock, elaborately pleated and gathered on the breast and shoulders, corduroy breeches, blue stockings of very humble make, and boots that weighed some six pounds apiece.

George Doggett -- Gamekeeper

Old William

For over fifty years, man and boy, Old William had worked on the same farm for the same family, and when warmed by a spirit of rivalry, combined with cider, could tell of ploughing matches in which he had taken his part, and how, at the age of twelve, he had " druv 'es vurrow" in a match and won the prize, "a gould zuv'rin," and how he " cum back to Westcombe wi' vlying ribbins."

Many were the quaint stories told of Old William, and he enjoyed a reputation for shrewdness which may or may not have been the outcome of his utter simplicity. Certain it is that no one could have invented half the queernesses attributed to him, for if you mentioned Old William to the Vicar, the Doctor, or his employer, Mr. Rickhays, each had some tale to tell in which he was the sufferer.

Ah!" the Vicar would say, with a twinkle in his eye, " William Mitchell ;—you want to know if he can do up a garden ? Yes! Oh, yes ! I borrowed him for a day or two. The first day he did very well,—but then we never left him ; the second day we trusted him alone, and found our asparagus beds,—the best in the county," said the Vicar plaintively, " trenched over two spades deep, and William burning all the plants which he shewed us with pride, as 'mazin strong couch."

Then the Doctor would chime in with " grand man for a horse, sir ; if you want to sell a horse, send

Old William. I sent him once to Axminster Fair with a capital cob, for which I wanted thirty guineas, and I planned, too, exactly, how I would spend that money. In about an hour, who should I see coming down the road, but Old William, with the bridle in his hand and the saddle on his head ; you could have knocked me down with a feather. He came on quite placidly, and said, "'Es de-a-d, an' I' ve zold 'es zkin for a zov'rin." It was quite true, the cob had died suddenly on the road, and William had promptly knocked him down to the highest bidder.

But ask Rickhays there, how they treated William on his jubilee.   Thus appealed to, Mr. Rickhays would tell, amidst much laughter, how on the completion of his fifty years of service, they cast about how they might treat Old William, and sent him to the sea (which, although he had lived within twelve miles of, he had never seen), with well-lined pockets and strict injunctions to keep his eyes open and observe everything. Old William set off; the following morning became to be interviewed, and relate his experiences. To the query of "Well, William, and how did you enjoy yourself?" he replied, "'Mazin well, thank yew kindly, zir. They've a deal better zider to Zeaton than they 'a' got to Westcombe." Nothing further could be extracted from William in reference to his expedition, but it transpired that the Red Lion being in the line of route, William had there settled himself, and only moved to return to Westcombe; thus it was thatOld William, having as it were travelled, and being skilled in horticultural matters, and cunning in horseflesh, was elected by acclamation as *President of the Symposia;* held at the Blue Cow.

Now the tap-room of the above, where the sayings and doings of this bucolic neighbourhood were criticised and discussed,partook of the nature of a convivial club, of which the members were the Westcombe villagers ; that their conviviality was produced by—to the uninitiated— immoderate libations of sour cider, made the conviviality none the less real; it only caused wonder to the onlookers how year after year they could possibly survive the process, and it was a matter of no little moment to the community that "Varmer Passons had raised 'es zhepherd on a zhillun a week," and also that " Muster Green to Hill Top Farm had lost a cow through being choked by a turmut;'" but to get a real excitement, an interest in their very ordinary lives outside the usual routine, and yet connected with one of their order, caused a buzz of pleasant anticipation to pervade the tap-room of the Blue Cow.

Joe Butt In Trouble

The story of the encounter between George Doggett and Joe Butt had leaked out thus: on Joe's arrival at his cottage, after his unfortunate night watch, he sneaked quietly into bed without awakening Mrs. B., but the morning's light revealed to her acute perceptions the

31

aesthetic blues and greens which Doggett's cudgel had painted on the too susceptible countenance of her Joseph. Now blues and greens had long been associated in the mind of Mrs. Butt with taprooms and rampant cattle of an azure tint ; therefore, without further prelude, slie plunged into the matter by asking, in a tone of fine irony, " How many qua-a-arts it took to geun that purty ve-ace."

Now Joe feared nothing human except his wife, and of her, her tongue, which, through long practice and an intimate acquaintance with his weak places, could pierce through every joint in his harness, he had a most uncommon dread; therefore, in an injured tone, he explained that the matter could not be looked at through the medium of" qua-arts," but was honestly gained in the pursuit of his legitimate occupation.Still incredulous, his wife observed, " Efzettin in a ditch at a zhillun a night cun gi' 'ee a veace like that'm, you'm better bide to whoam along o' we." Many a lie had Joe Butt told the wife of his bosom to account for occasional outbreaks, but to have his virtue assailed when for once he happened to be in the right, overcame his prudence and reticence, and he gave her a detailed account of the adventure, with strongly emphasised outbursts of indignation, by no means lessened by the soreness of his head and his wife's jeers, and further revenging himself for her unjust suspicians by dire threats if she repeated "aught about it".

Mrs. Butt, though impressed by the evident truth of the narration, showed her contempt for the threats by rushing off then and there, on her pattens, and bonnetless, to relatel to her special cronies, under the seal of inviolable secrecy, a highly embellished account of the adventure ; and this is how every man, woman, and child in Westcombe by twelve o'clock knew that George Doggett and Joe Butt had had a tremendous encounter with poachers, that Joe Butt had received his death blow from at least four different men, and that his wife and seven children contemplated the position of a widow and orphans with a serenity which those who had lately seen Mrs. Butt considered, under the circumstances, to be " most mazin."

The company at the Blue Cow on this auspicious and exciting occasion was both numerous and select. There, nearest the fire, in virtue of his office, sat Old William Mitchell in all the glory of a newly replenished pint and long clay pipe ; the babel of voices was loud but contradictory, for as none of them had been there, none could speak with authority. It was at this moment, timed doubtless with a full consciousness of their importance, and a certain striving after dramatic effect, that Sam Pitcher and John Fry, the two watchers, entered the room. " Ere they be! ere they be ! "was shouted and echoed by a score of throats,—" Tak a drap out o' my moog," was the almost universal request as they slowly walked up the

The Vicar
An important character in country life.

room ; but no, the solemnity of the occasion demanded full pints of their own, and being supplied, Sam Pitcher, as spokesman for self and partner, cast a patronising glance around, and remarked to the company generally, " There do zeem a zight o' volk here t' night." " Es zure," replied Old William, with a wave of his pipe, "us be main glad as 'e be com'd, us d'want to hear 'bout they poarchers."

Amidst a hush of breathless expectation, Sam replied very solemnly, " there war'nt no poarchers." This was too much—a moment's silence, and then a universal cry went up "W'at? no poarchers !" " No," said Sam. " I'll tell 'ee all 'bout it. Jan Vry an' me 'greed wi Jarge Doggett to watch a 'long o' he an Joe Butt vor a zhillun, didn' us, Jan ? " Appealing to John Fry, who sat next him. " Us did, an little 'nuff too," replied his partner. " Zo 'twor," was sympathetically chorussed from every corner of the room, and further emphasised by another expressive wave of the pipe from Old William, " 'twer past twelve, an I hears a zhout from Jarge, an' up Jan an I runs, an us zees two men a vightin."

"They was layin it on too," observed John Fry parenthetically. " Specially Jarge," put in Sam. " Specially Jarge," corroborated John Fry. "Moon wer hid, an you couldn' zee your han afore 'e, but we zays gi' ut un, Jarge." "Ay, us did," said John Fry. "An then moon zhined out an us zees Joe Butt a-dressin Jarge," and,

George Doggett -- Gamekeeper

Typical Poacher
Adapted from *I Walked by Night*

interrupted John Fry, "Jarge a dressin 'e." "Zo 'said Sam", again taking up the parable, " Jarge zays, zays 'e, wy, Joe, be that thee ? " " Es zure," zays Joe.

"Wy, Jarge, I thort 'e wor a poarcher." "Jarge a poarcher !" came in a chorus from the assembled company. The joke was so intense that Old William ordered another pint on the strength of it, an indiscretion of which he had not been guilty for many a day, and chuckling softly to himself, repeated at intervals throughout the evening, accompanied by sympathetic waves of his pipe, "Jarge a poarcher." Thus ended the episode which caused much merriment to Westcombe generally, and a not inconsiderable addition to the nightly takings of host **Trout.**

George Doggett Was An Important Figure In the Community.

4

WESTCOMBE MANOR.

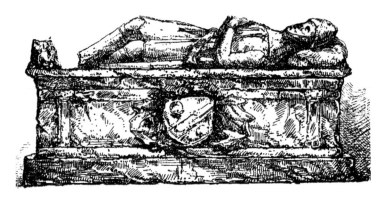

Stone Carving of a certain Geoffrey de Wynheard, and Dorothy, his wife.

This is located in the Church.

CHAPTER IV.

WESTCOMBE MANOR.

THE Hall possessed no special characteristics other than that of a country gentleman's residence of the nineteenth century, which by careful suppression of decorative details had become architecturally common-place; and yet it was well known to have seen stirring times, for associated with other Squires of like sentiment, the Wynheards had been out with Monmouth, and given and taken shrewd blows, and when that ill-fated rising fell to pieces the Wynheards and Westcombe very nearly fell to pieces , with it; but the old line and house were spared, the one to grace our story, the other to be rebuilt, or partially so thrice, for even yet there peeped out here and there traceries and broken bits of stone ornament, once the pride of a noble residence, further endorsed by the lofty ivy-twined chimney shafts, spared by changes which amounted to vandalism, which had crushed out all interest and beauty from the building below. This is only to ourselves, for he was a bold man who would proclaim in the hearing of Westcombe, at least, that the Hall was other than a thing of beauty ; but what it lacked in outward decoration was amply compensated by the air of comfort that pervaded its interior, from the lofty entrance hall, through the oak panelled dining room, upstairs and down, to the Squire's special sanctum, where he held consultation with his bailiff, or dispensed justices' justice, there was a warmth and substantiality which betokened a pocket at ease.

The house, sheltered from the east by wood and hill, was, as are many of our West Country seats, on a gentle rise ; thus, whilst the view was limited, this very limitation enhanced the feeling of proprietorship, for on three sides the Wynheards owned the land as far as eye could see ; very charming, too, was the outlook over slope and hollow, fern. and brake, glade following glade, until warming with the western glow, far away shimmers the ever restless sea, now in shadow, now in light, yet once again in shadow, till the eye, wearying, of its changing mood, turns for rest to the famous woods of Westcombe.

Such surroundings made as pleasant a home as man could wish, and as this was the Squire's opinion, in which his wife concurred, their poorer

The Squire & His Lady

43

neighbours enjoyed the benefit of a resident landlord who loved his people, and whom his people loved. That the bond of affection was a strong one, partaking almost of a patriarchal nature was manifest, for the village squabbles and disputes which the vicar failed to arrange were submitted to the Squire, and usually adjusted to the ' satisfaction of the contending parties.

The Squire, the Lord of Westcombe Manor, was a gentle-man from the crown of his head to the sole of his foot, a straight-forward, liberal-minded, free-handed English man unselfish yet practical, who tried to do his duty by his neighbour, was worshipped by his dependants, loved by his equals, and envied by not a few who thought themselves his superiors; add to this that he was well set up, stood five feet eleven inches in his stockings, rode thirteen stone, was a notable authority on all sport, and you will see that " Wynheard of Westcombe" was a man to be envied.

The Squire's Lady

Of the "Squire's lady " we need say no more than that she fulfilled her duties admirably, and had presented her husband fourteen years before the date of this story with a son, whom his father christened John, and whom, as "Jack Wynheard," we shall follow through many of these pages.

44

Urn in Church

The little society in the village consisted of the Vicar—
a college friend of the Squire—who, having no children,
taught Jack his humanities, and loved the boy as his
own, and the "Doctor," who was, according to his own
statement, the hardest worked and worst paid man in
the county, but, notwithstanding these drawbacks,
enjoyed life and sipped many of its sweets.

Little Jack

Of little Jack it is not too much to say that he was unspoilable, if he had not been this record would have lacked one of its most pleasing features—a lovable boy, bright and intelligent, if somewhat old-fashioned : a spice of the Squire's thoroughness and straight-forwardness, tempered with his mother's gentleness ; like his father, he was worshipped by the servants, whom he wheedled in the most barefaced manner, from Mrs. Round, the cook, who, in tortoiseshell spectacles and cunningly contrived front, blest his little heart and gave him unlimited cakes—to old Binnell, the butler, who provided him with surreptitious dessert at every opportunity. But his special ally was Doggett, rarely a day passing that Jack was not at the Lodge, or in company with the keeper, and it was evidence of the trust that the Squire reposed in his man that he allowed his son to associate so freely with him.

Doggett valued the trust, and never betrayed it, but naturally imbued him with his own tastes, so that at fourteen years of age, Jack Wynheard knew as much about birds and beasts, dogs and traps, and could shoot as straight as most young men double his age.

The village proper, guiltless of drains and redolent of odours, was just what the Doctor called it, " a dear little insanitary spot," a mixture of red tiled and yellow thatched cottages, charmingly clustered amongst gardens and orchards, pig styes and cowsheds, with fields between so vivid in their green-ery that they threw into perfect relief the rich red cattle which the conservatism of the cream-loving approved.

Westcombe villagers only allowed them to keep. Then there was the village inn—" The Blue Cow,"—where the villagers—or rather the male portion—did nightly congregate ; but as their wives knew their whereabouts, and got them out of the way whilst they put the children to bed, little harm was done.

Opposite the inn, on the crest of the hill forming the crown of the village, stands the church. Few, per-haps, of my readers know how much the village churches are interwoven with the lives of the country folk—there were they christened and married ; there will they be buried ; there also lie those dear to them, as well as many of their village companions—the churchyard is a book of memories, the stones its pages.

Westcombe, like many of these West Country churches, was structurally interesting, and well re-paid a visit.   Beside yews there existed a few old monuments, two magnificent three stone coffins, and a crusader, whom the Wynheards claimed as an heir-loom, a sort of treasure-trove, and at once elevated into an early ancestor ; indeed, people of liberal minds went so far as to see a likeness to the present Squire ; but, as the crusader had lost a nose, and centuries of exposure had whittled down his once expressive fea-tures, the resemblance could scarcely be termed a striking one.

Inside, the church was old-fashioned, as happily the hand of the restorer had been held; this was partly due to the excellence of the old oak—Westcombe grown—with which it was filled, and partly to the wisdom of the Squire, who, with the villagers, preferred old associations and high-backed pews to modern innovations and low benches. Of course the Squire's pew, as became the Lord of the Manor, was square, comfortable, well lined, hassocked, and carpeted throughout, and further tastefully embellished with mural decorations descriptive of the virtues of bygone Wynheards, foremost amongst them being a stone carving of a certain Geoffrey de Wynheard, and Dorothy, his wife, in ruffles and strict devotional attitudes, with attendant cherub, who, by his powerful trumpeting, caused in the mind of little Jack weekly speculation as to the ultimate dilatability of stone cheeks.

There were incongruities, too, in the little church, and its services, which would make the hair of many a High Church parson of the present day stand on end ; but custom had habituated Westcombe folk to Westcombe ways, and nobody doubted their strict orthodoxy. There was an old three-decker pulpit, consisting of a square box for the clerk, another above it, with a reading-desk, and a third higher still, from whence to deliver the sermon; and it added much to the impressiveness of the discourse that a sounding-board, swung overhead, of a size and shape admirably adapted for the immediate extinction of the preacher, should the fastening unfortunately give way.

Other Characters

The village choir — pure Westcombe — fearfully and wonderfully composed, was a strong point in the services ; they sat in the gallery opposite the pulpit, the instrumental part consisting of a bass viol, two clarionets, a violin, and two flutes—the tuning continuing without intermission till the entrance of the Vicar into the reading-desk, was considered in the light of an opening voluntary ; their repertoire was limited, but what matter ?

Everyone knew the " Old Hundredth," and sang with all their hearts. The leader of this unique orchestra—one Caleb Cross—was a character : when not engaged in gentle dalliance with his muse, he filled the important post of village tailor ; but his one recreation, and apparently the sole ambition of his life— for the fit of his garments was excruciating—was the production of sounds, more or less harmonious, from his bass viol; long companionship had, so to speak, welded Caleb and his instrument together ; whether the bass viol had grown like Caleb, or Caleb like the bass viol, I cannot say, but that a certain marked and extraordinary resemblance existed between the two was certain, and nature had assisted by so shaping Caleb's legs, that they adjusted themselves to the curves of his instrument in a way that surely no legs ever did adjust themselves before or since.

A vigorous young woman—by name Charity Cripps—led the voices with a confidence and power that made up for other deficiences. There was no nervousness about her ; she made her attack and led her choir with a verve that would have done credit to a. prima-donna.

The Vicar was long-suffering and easy going, but once a year, at least, complained of there being no vestry, and that it was unduly stretching the canon of " doing all things decently and in order," when, Sunday after that on Sunday, he was required to robe and disrobe in the garish light, of day—that is, full before his congregation ; but Farmer Worzel, his churchwarden, said, soothingly, " Lor, zir, do'ant yow mind ; volk d'like to zee 'ee gettin in an out o' they things."

Still, in time, revolutionary ideas penetrated even to Westcombe, and Mrs. Wynheard persuaded the Squire to build a vestry, much to the regret, of the congregation, who felt themselves defrauded of what they had learned to consider an interesting part of the service.

This record would be obviously incomplete did we omit mention of Matthew Mattock, a man naturally endowed for the post of sexton and parish clerk.

Matthew looked the part and lived it—a tall saturnine man, as was fit for church-yards—he welcomed the coming, that is, officiated at christenings, or speeded the parting guest by performing his duties at funerals with an air inimitable in its appropriateness. Matthew, too, had no false pride in associating himself with the Vicar in ecclesiastical duties, but invariably said '' we," such as—" we'm goin' to have a christening or funeral," "we'm goin'to preach for the missionarys," and I don't think that honest Matthew ever thought that the Vicar had much to do with it. Gifts in the way of broad-cloth, which once had graced the vicarial back, framed Matthew into a sort of far-away replica of the Vicar, which may perhaps account for this peculiarity ; but there was also the importance of the post in the eyes and ears of Westcombe, for sure it was that they all considered their clerk's *A-a-a-a-men* a vocal effort of the highest excellence, and an integral part of the service so important that its suppression would have been a rubrical schism in no way to be tolerated.

George Doggett -- Gamekeeper

OUT ON THE ESTATE

5
THE PLEASURES
OF THE CHASE.

Animal Poacher
The Fox after any morsel to be found.
Adapted from *British Mammals*, Archibald Thorburn, BPH

CHAPTER V.
THE PLEASURES OF THE CHASE.

Vor 'tis my delight o' a zhiny night,
In the zeason o' the ye-a-a-a-ar."

SO SINGS the poacher; can we wonder at it ? Yet it adds not a little to the excitement that there is reasonable probability of being caught redhanded, and hauled before the Squire, with certain pains and penalties thereto attached.

But Squires are discerning, and by no means lack the milk of human kindness. So the pains and penalties are adjusted for the moral obliquity of the offender.

Of poachers there are many varieties Firstly there is the man, who from want, or a longing for food other than rusty bacon, throws discretion to the winds, and despite tearful remonstrances from half starved wife, responds to the eager, glistening eyes of hungry children.

So it is with our old friend Reynard; he poaches to live, rather than lives to poach, and if   he does mistake a fat pullet for a young pheasant, or whip off a newly dropped lamb, we are lenient to his shortcomings, for it is the law of self-preservation.

Then there is your poacher who poaches for the love of it, for whom the pursuit of game has an irresistible fascination, who has reduced it almost to a science, or a fine art; to whom the snaring of hares, netting of partridges, tickling of trout, seems a necessity of existence. He lives to poach, and does not poach to live.

Lastly, there is your thorough scoundrel, who caring nothing for the sport, with plenty of honest work awaiting him, if only he chooses to do it, will rather join thirty other scoundrels as bad as himself to sweep the neighbouring preserves of bipeds and quadrupeds, stone and bludgeon some lonely keeper or watcher, and boast of his prowess.

Happily this development of modern civilisation was unknown at Westcombe. Hitherto the yokels on whom the Squire had sat in judgment belonged to the second class, for both he and Mrs. Wynheard took good care that no starving labourers were to be found within reach of the manor. But in the matter of pheasants the Squire was keen, and he directed Doggett to organise night-watches as a precaution against further loss. A week passed without renewal of the attempt, so the extra men were withdrawn, and the usual

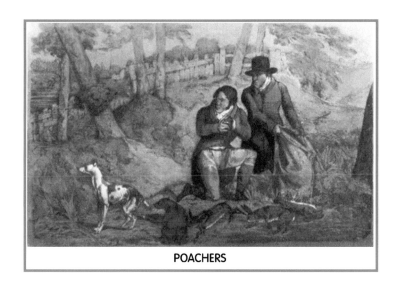

POACHERS

Doggett had expected *this* scene, but,
in fact,
there was only one poacher.

routine of an evening walk and morning round was re-established.

Still Doggett's suspicions, once thoroughly aroused, were difficult to remove, and he found himself suddenly waking with imaginary gunshots ringing in his ears, and showed other evidence of a mind not quite at ease within itself. Whether these nocturnal disturbances were the outcome of mental perturbation, or an inward sign of the outward application of Joe Butt's cudgel, I am unable to determine ; but sure it was that they existed, and were a source of great disquietude to their victim.

After many such false alarms, Doggett again awaked with the sound of a gun in his ears; and inclined at first to believe that it was another deception, he was preparing to fall asleep, when a second report, about which there could be no mistake, thoroughly aroused him. To spring out of bed, dress himself, seize a heavy stick, grope his way downstairs and into the darkness of the night, was a matter of a few minutes; he would more readily have faced, single-handed, any number of men, than meet the Squire with another tale of despoiled coverts unavenged.

Once in the open air, his knowledge of the locality enabled him to travel rapidly, though heavy clouds obscured the moon ; with a returning gleam came a shot, clear and startling- in the still midnight This time, without doubt, the sound proceeded from the Holly Wood. With an oath, which might fairly be condoned, Doggett dashed down a side path, and running swiftly but carefully, reached the wicket gate opening into the plantation. Here great care was necessary, for, with all his pluck, Doggett was not deficient in the instinct of self-preservation, and as such unwelcome visitors rarely came alone, he hoped that " the conscience which makes cowards of all" would scatter them at the first alarm. The light was uncertain, therefore caution was necessary if he wished to effect a capture.

Creeping stealthily, hiding himself as the moon broke forth, he made his way to the centre of the wood, close to the feeding sheds, where he knew the birds mostly congregated, and again the gun sounded—this time very near.

There's another groaned Doggett, tightening the grasp on his stick, and walking rapidly forward. A few steps brought him in sight of a man, a stranger, standing alone, with a gun in one hand and a newly-killed pheasant in the other.

" I'm danged," said the keeper, quite breathless with exasperation, " only one o' 'em;" and with a shout to imaginary John Frys and Joe Butts, he rushed straight for the marauder. With ordinary luck the capture might have been effected then and there, for the intruder was so taken by surprise that he stood for a moment helpless and irresolute, but Doggett, catching his foot in a bramble, stumbled, and falling heavily,

Doggett Advances With Stick Raised

rolled over and over almost to the feet of the poacher, who, turning, fled down a side path at a speed which soon widened the distance between them.

Gathering himself together, Doggett regained his feet, and though badly shaken, and lots of run knocked out of him, set his teeth hard, and stripped off his coat for what he felt would be an effort such as he had never before been called upon to make; following at such speed as the winding paths and insufficient light permitted, he gained the edge of the wood, and the open country lying before him.

Doggett saw his antagonist running easily— gun in hand—half-way across a field ; to leap the fence, every muscle tense and sinew strung, and to set himself to his work in real earnest was for the keeper now a necessity; at first he thought he could race his man down. He quickened his pace but the the poacher responded, until a chase of half a mile found them with their relative positions unchanged.

The keeper, despairing of overtaking the poacher—for they had long overstepped the Westcombe boundary, and were nearing the river— pounded doggedly along, with.the determination, as he muttered to himself, to run "till I do drop," and indeed he was not far from that consummation ; for meadow after meadow had been crossed, ditch after ditch waded—they were too exhausted to leap— and fence after fence crashed through, leaving them two mud-splashed, miserable-looking beings.

Those of my readers who have seen a spent fox, with draggled brush and lolling tongue, make its last effort at the end of an exhausting run, can picture to themselves the condition. of the poacher. Turning round, like a wild animal brought to bay, he saw Doggett—in little better plight than himself, tumble head first into the ditch at his feet; here. then, was a chance—one blow with the weapon he carried, and the keeper would trouble him no more. Did the thought cross his mind ? If so, he thrust it from him.

With a half laugh at Doggett's predicament— for even his own desperately evil case could not entirely suppress his sense of the ludicrous—he looked at the river, descended the bank, **and slowly entering the water,** began to cross as Doggett extricated himself from the ditch, with all the run shaken out of him, and his bellicose intentions supplanted by a feeling of wonder at his opponent's generosity. For a time all went well though the river, swollen by the November rains, ran dark and sullen ; the moon's rays glimmered on the surface, than the poacher might well have turned from.

Bitterly cold was the hungry water as it hurried onwards, and only by the height of the wave, as it rose up the bodyof the staggering man, could the strength of the current be gauged; for a moment

Doggett stood, breathlessly, watching ; then his better nature and kindliness reasserted themselves, for, knowing the treacherous depths and force of the stream, he could well estimate the risk of the enterprise. " Cum back !" he hoarsely shouted, " cum back, an I'll let 'ee go, vor zure ; do 'ee cum back," he entreated, " or you'm be drownded." A shake of the head was the only reply.

The force of the stream increased as the middle of the river was gained, and the water rose higher and higher ; the luckless poacher began to waver, he half turned, in response to the keeper's agonised entreaties—too late—with a splash and a struggle he fell, and was swept into deep water. Quickly he sank, as quickly reappeared, striking out for the opposite bank; unfortunately, he had miscalculated his strength, for within a few feet of the side he again sank, once more rose, and made his last effort. For a moment it seemed as if he might win home, but, quite spent, he disappeared a third time—carried away like a straw.

A Foolish Act ?

Doggett—oblivious of the fact that he was no swimmer—was in the stream, and half-way across, watching for the reappearance of his late opponent. The current was running strongly towards Doggett, and just as he despaired of success, the body was swept

63

River in Flood
The Poacher almost loses his life and is rescued by
George Doggett.

within a yard of him ; rushing forward he lost his foot-
ing, but seized the clothing of the drowning man. He
struggled hard, but the weight of the body and strength
of the current were too much; he rolled over and under, still retaining his hold of the poacher

Visions of his cottage—his simple, honest life—
the kind Squire—little Jack—all passed rapidly before
him; then, for a moment—oblivion. But the keeper was
a strong man, in the prime of life ; so, rallying his
fast failing powers, he made one desperate effort; his
foot touched the bottom—a flash of hope ; another step,
again the ground ;   the current was less strong, the
water shallower, and at last, dazed and exhausted, yet
with a dim consciousness of success, George Doggett
dragged himself and his prize out of the water.

The   Rescue

Happily, the bank was low and easy of access; Pant-
ing, lay, Doggett, till he gathered strength to attempt
the restoration of the poacher. The immersion had
been a short one, yet it was a long time before Doggett
succeeded in partially restoring the half-drowned
man. Great persuasion was necessary to induce him
to attempt to walk, but at last he began to move slowly
towards the Lodge.

The journey back was terrible; it proved nearly fatal to the poacher, who many times lapsed into partial unconsciousness, until Doggett had to carry the all but inanimate body in his arms.   The effort was a severe one for the keeper, but it probably saved him from the consequences of his own immersion. Never was man more grateful than he, when, depositing his unfortunate prisoner in a chair in front of the fire, which was easily rekindled, brewing him a stiff tumbler, and taking one himself, he prepared to spend the night as best he might.

It was evident that the poacher was quite exhausted, but Doggett hoped, as the warmth crept over him, he might rally, and be restored to complete consciousness; to this end he placed him in his own bed, wrapping him in a hot blanket, and piled on all the clothes he could.   For a time reaction restored the man sufficiently to answer a few questions, but the exertions of the night, with severe cold and shock from immersion, reasserted themselves, and he appeared, even to Doggett's unpractised eye, to be very poorly.

Many an anxious look did the keeper turn from his capture to the old clock, which, to his excited imagination, relentlessly ticked chance after chance off the life of the poacher; there he lay—a man of Doggett's own age, but slighter build, thin and poorly fed—still more poorly clad, for his clothes scarce hung together in their threadbare condition.

The Bank Was Low
Doggett managed to drag the Poacher
from the water.

The face, so far as could be seen, was an intelligent one, but unshorn, unshaven, and sick, no opinion could be formed as to what manner of man he was.

Poachers Ferreting

6
THE NURSING
OF
WILL

Village Life Went On
But Will the Poacher was very ill.

CHAPTER VI.

THE NURSING OF WILL.

THE grey dawn of a chill November morning found Doggett still beside the bed of the stricken man. The pallor of shock and exhaustion was now replaced by the flush of fever, whilst the intervals of consciousness became less and less, until as the dull light forced its way through the chinks in the closed shutters, all sequence of ideas was lost, and he lay moaning and muttering—muttering and moaning—till Doggett's hair fairly rose with the fear that he might die before assistance could be obtained.

The trials of that night were never forgotten by the keeper; the fitful wailings of disordered fancy—by turns appealing, argumentative, imploring-— the sudden snatch for intelligence rapidly passing away; the feeble cry of bodily prostration; all this so worked upon his feelings, that, if it were not for very shame for his manhood, George Doggett would, there and then, have left his unfortunate prisoner to wrestle alone with the enemy, in whose strong grasp he was now so surely held.

It required little medical skill to foretell that the poacher was sorely smitten, almost, if not quite, to the death ; that his body, wasted with starvation and want, could ill struggle against the shock of exposure and immersion, and Doggett, in whom anxiety had now overcome every other feeling, hailed the appearance of Joe Butt with an outburst of delight surprising to the recipient.

A few words sufficed to acquaint. Joe with the experiences of the night and the gravity of the situation. At quick speed he passed through the village, to the doctor's house—the bearer of an urgent message from Doggett. The doctor was at home, and, happily, an early man, so soon stood by the bedside of the luckless poacher. As succinctly as he could, Doggett reviewed the night's adventure to the attentive surgeon, who, examining his patient, observed, " Poor fellow ! seems a young man : who is he ?"
" I don't know un," replied Doggett, " 'e zays e's name's Murrill—Will Murrill, born down Barnstaple way, but he've tramp'd about a deal."

Again the doctor examined him closely, and shaking his head, said, in answer to the keeper's anxious looks, "He's in a bad way" he said, "therefore we must work hard to keep him alive." "Just so," said the Vicar vaguely. "What do you propose ? "

Now if this worthy clergyman had a weakness, it was that of considering himself specially gifted in the way of medicine ; physic the people he would, and many a tussle had the Doctor and he had over his proclivities in this direction. So when the wily Doctor replied, " I should like you to tell me what you think best to be done," the flattery was so delicate and subtle, that the good man could hardly resist the temptation; but here was a case of a gravity far beyond that with which he was accustomed to deal. It was a small matter, comparatively, to administer peppermint potions for "windy spavins," or blue pill for a flagrant example of the "boil," but to suggest a treatment for a drowned—- or a nearly drowned—man was beyond him ; so the Vicar humm'd and haa'd, until the Doctor, in return for an excellent pigeon pie—into which he had made free inroad-- came to the rescue, and said, " We must have a nurse—a capable woman— who can do anything."   " Of course, of course," replied the other ; " who will you have ?"

" Nancy Nert," promptly replied the Doctor. "A most unfit, unregenerate person," said the Vicar ; she never goes to church !"   " Oh, yes, she does," replied the Doctor, with a chuckle; " She goes on dole day, for she told me only last week the bread you gave her was so bad she had 'the colict' every time she took it." But the Vicar would not smile; he had been worsted in a verbal encounter with Nancy a few days before.

Nancy Nert is the only woman in the parish who has the time and the knowledge," proceeded the Doctor. " Well! well!" said the Vicar, half-resignedly, " but she has no moral sense."

" That doesn't matter a pin at present," said the Doctor, " as there is no chance of this man regaining his moral or any other sense for the next ten days." "I told her," said the Vicar, still with a sore feeling, " that she was a bad example to the parish; and she was pert— very pert."

" What did she say ?" inquired the Doctor.

" She told me every tub must stand on its own bottom; and when I replied, 'Yes, Nancy, but suppose it has no bottom ?'—' set it on the rims,' said she. What can you do with a woman who has no more idea of the fitness of things than to bandy words with her clergyman ? Still, as you say, I don't know anyone else, and we had better employ her. Of course you can have soup, wine, and anything else you require." " Very well, then," said the Doctor, satisfied with having engaged the Vicar's active co-operation, " I will call at the Hall and tell the Squire all about it, and we must do our best to save this poor fellow."

In due course, Nancy was installed head nurse, and a capital one she made, for if her moral sense was absent, her common sense was all there. But, in spite of the most anxious care and attention, the sands of

Nancy Nert, Nurse

poor Murrill's life ran so low, that the Doctor was almost inclined to give up the struggle, and it was only
the dire distress of Doggett that prevented him from
so doing. Murrill slowly recovered consciousness, and,
after weeks of watching, their anxious care was rewarded by such distinct improvement that recovery
seemed attainable.

Human nature is a strange compound of the
comprehensible and the incomprehensible — the lat-
ter usually predominating. Here was a human being—
an outcast-caught *flagrante delicto* (freely interpreted) with a pheasant in each pocket—and yet, because he happened to have been nearly drowned in
running away from the scene of his delinquencies,
sympathy took root, grew, and flourished, until its
branches overshadowed all the ne'er-do-well's previous misdeeds, converting his deserved mishap into
undeserved misfortune, his shiftless life into honest
struggles with adversity, and enwrapping him in such
an engaging covering of heroism, that the villagers
began to doubt whether poaching was the enormity
they had hitherto considered it, particularly if associated with unlimited soup and wine.

But the Squire, though he was sorry for Murrill,
was not the man to be led away by sentiment, and as

PHEASANTS OVER THE GUNS
After Rickman, from GAME BIRDS by Hugh B C Pollard.

week after week passed without that marked improvement which might be expected, he intimated
very plainly to the Doctor that he had had enough of
Will Murrill.

7

A DAY'S

MIXED SHOOTING.

Wild Ducks
After Edward A Wilson

CHAPTER VII.

A DAY'S MIXED SHOOTING.

IT must not be supposed that the sporting proclivities of the Squire were kept in abeyance during this anxious and exciting time, for although affairs at the Lodge were engrossing to those immediately in attendance upon Murrill, their usual duties were required of Doggett and the under-keepers. The Holmwood, too, in spite of its previous depletion, yielded a full quota, showing that either little harm had been done, or that the inflow of birds from neighbouring shootings was not unknown.

One of the greatest charms of a day over Westcombe was the variety of game that could be shot, and to test this the Squire one evening sent for Doggett, and said, "I met Mr. Colyton this morning, and he told me of a mixed bag they made one day over Chudbury. I want to try and beat it. What can we do to-morrow ?" Touched on his tenderest point, Doggett replied disdainfully, " I heard tell o' that bag, but we can do to Westcombe every bit zo well as they can do to Chudbury, vor 'tisn't zo

81

terrible grand a place vor zhooting: ef Master Jack'll rackon up we'll zee."

Jack, all eyes and ears at the thought of a day's shooting, prepared his fingers. " Pattridges, veasants, hares, rabbuts," began Doggett; four, checked Jack promptly. " A woodcock, may be two in Holmwood, and a snipe in they withys," — up rose another thumb, making six. " Then I zeed some ducks vlying up river this very evenin', an Joe do tell I he've zeed zome teal an' widgin."—Nine came from the marker. " Any plover?" asked the Squire, " I heerd one or two whistlin' round Muster Worzel's plough ground, we might get one," said Doggett doubtfully, "but they'm main zhy. Peewits and a queest o'course." " Jack snipe ?" queried the Squire. "I ha'n't zeed one t'year," said Doggett; " anyway, ef we get all they, it's better nor Chudbury bag." " All right, then," said the Squire, "tell Joe, and bring the retriever, two spaniels, and the old pointer, and we'll meet you at the split oak at eight to-morrow morning, or the ducks will be going down again." As the "we" included Jack, his delight knew no bounds ; all the more that the Squire told him to bring his gun—a light piece made specially for him—and he went to bed to dream of impossible bags of gigantic live ducks, whose quacking grew so loud; it was seven o'clock , and breakfast would soon be ready.

It was a beautiful frosty morning, a whitish

RABBIT (THORBURN)

Rabbit Warren
There were rabbits in plenty

83

mist obscuring the distance, but there was a promise of sunshine, and the air felt exhilarating with just that freshness and hope so dear to ardent sportsmen. A twenty minutes' walk brought them to the riven oak, once the glory of Westcombe, now only a shattered giant, pathetic in its destruction ; grouped round the base, forming a pretty picture—were the keepers with the dogs. "Good morning," said the Squire, in response to a general salute, "just the morning for us, I think."

" Now, Doggett"—taking his gun— "we will go right up the river and try for a duck before they go down." Jack in a seventh heaven of delight trotted behind in amicable converse with the keepers and dogs.

A walk of half a mile brought them to the boundary of Westcombe, close to the river. With a caution born of experience, the careless talk and open order were exchanged for silence and Indian file, the Squire leading ; under cover of a high wattle fence they gained the bank, but a careful survey up and down stream failed to detect any waterfowl.

They had already turned to work down the river, when Doggett, whose restless eyes seemed to scan earth, air, and water, at one and the same time, said in a hurried whisper, " Crope down, zir, crope down, there'm three coming right down stream." In a moment the company sank noiselessly under the fence, awaiting breathlessly the oncoming of the unsuspiicious birds, which could be seen coming across. When they reached the fence the Squire fired, bringing down two of the birds.

In a few moments the retriever had deposited the birds with Doggett, who announced them to be widgeon, and as duck were certain to be found lower down, the commencement was an auspicious one. No time was lost, but it was a full half mile before a duck and mallard rose just out of shot, to drop about four hundred yards lower. " There'm more birds there, or they wouldn't drop like that," said Doggett, "they'm in Withy Pool." "Yes," said the Squire, "and Jack and I will go down the fence, and through the gate we shall just drop on them."

The Squire, Jack, Doggett, and the retriever hastened forwards, and soon reached the hedge which hid them from the river. Here Doggett, peeping through a gap, announced five ducks on the pond, within range. As they reached the gate, the five birds rose in the air, in the hope. of finishing their disturbed seance nearer the sea. "Now, Jack, steady," said the Squire, and as Jack responded by killing the nearest, the Squire supplemented his previous performance with another right and left, which, as the birds rose not twenty yards away, was not so brilliant an effort as to call for comment.

" There," said the Squire, " we need spend no more time here, but work through the withys for a

Woodcock May Be Found
After a painting by Philip Rickman

snipe."

As they crossed the meadows, the old pointer was let loose, and drawing carefully, he came to a point at a little spring in the field where a few rushes and unusual greenery betokened warmth. Rapidly walking up they flushed two full snipe—the Squire fired both barrels, but as he had forgotten to reload with snipe shot, and the birds rose wild, they went on their way uninjured. "Serve me right" said the Squire, " I can't kill snipe with a duck gun, but" turning to Jack, "we should be able to kill a snipe or two here".

In a few minutes the beaters startled a snipe ; again the Squire missed, to his own disgust and the aston ishment of Doggett, for the Squire very seldom did miss. " Too quick," he muttered. The next bird rose nicely for Jack, and to Doggett's delight not less than his own, he knocked it over; then the Squire killed three in succession, and at the last corner a little Jack snipe was sprung, but its curious doubles and twists proved too much for our young sportsman, and it was left for the Squire, who dropping it said, " If we can only find a teal we are safe."

"There's the rush ponds where you killed they dree birds last year, they'm as likely as not, an' there is teal about," said Doggett. " Come on, then," said the Squire. So to the rush ponds they went, and very cautiously, too, for teal are wary and wide-

WILD DUCKS (AFTER RICKMAN)

Wild Duck on Pond

88

SNIPE SHOOTING

89

awake, and fly with amazing speed; there, sure enough, they were, doing credit to Doggett's pre-science, four lovely birds, with their brown, green, and white plumage glistening in the sun.

They rose before Jack and the Squire got within thirty yards of the pool; the shot was a long and difficult one—a full sixty yards—but the Squire had taken the precaution of loading with cartridge in one barrel, and two of the four fell fluttering into the rushes. " I know'd there was teal," said the keeper, exultingly, " an' now we'm zure to beat they Chudbury chaps." It was only eleven o'clock, and already they had gathered five out of a possible thirteen. " Now, for a plover," said the Squire. So away they trudged across the estate,—picking up a hare and a rabbit or two—to a remote corner, where, in a plough ground of Farmer Worzel's, infested with wireworm, plover loved to congregate and hold high revel. The ques-tion was how to get them. Golden plover are amongst the most astute of bipeds, and always keep sentries on the watch ; it is therefore impossible to stalk them. Know-ing this, the Squire suggested that Jack and he should each take a corner of the field, and lie hid in a ditch, whilst Doggett and the beaters were to shew themselves at the other end, so that if plover were on the fallow, they might fly over the guns.

This programme was carried out ; the Squire and Jack hid in the ditch, and the beaters commenced to walk the field. With the whistle so characteristic of plover, a small flock rose and went at an awful pace straight for the Squire, apparently certain for a shot they suddenly wheeled round in their usual criss-cross exasperating manner, showing their white underwings; in desperation, the Squire gave them a dose of" No. 4," and a view hallo, turning them towards Jack.

In a moment, the birds, some six or eight, were flying over his head faster than anything he had ever seen before; but he pointed his gun, pulled the trigger, and to the delight of the Squire and Doggett, and the unbounded admiration of the beaters, dropped one of the birds. It is hard to say which felt the greatest pride— the Squire, Doggett, or Jack— for let, me tell my unsophisticated readers that to kill a golden plover, in full flight, as it passes overhead, is a very difficult feat.

The day was yet young, and if the Holly Wood contained a cock or two, as Doggett prophesied, it was well to make sure of them before lunch time, for then the afternoon could be given up to partridges, or a few rabbits might be shot for the villagers, for the Squire was generous with his game.

George Doggett -- Gamekeeper

Arranging the beat, the Squire elected to go through the wood with Doggett and the spaniels, whilst Jack walked outside. The Holly Wood was a noted covert for cocks; it lay on a warm sloping bank with marshy bottom, through the centre of which trickled a little stream—here and there drives were cut, and the underwood was so thick and warm, that if the cocks were not there they ought to be.

Everything being arranged, the beat commenced, and the undergrowth was probed here and poked there, whilst the spaniels, with their busy sterns, working their hardest, fidgetted about to find a cock. Apparently he was not at home—until, at the end of the wood, in a little bosky dell, where a bubbling spring kept the grass green, and where a mass of dried bracken afforded a comfortable lodging, rose a long-billed bird dressed in rich browns and velvety blacks, with a coquettish morsel of white tipping the tail; it flew with a zig-zag flight, yet wonderful strength of wing, rapid and noiseless.

A storm of yells, " **Mark cock Mark cock**" came from the beaters' throats; the spaniels yelped in chorus, and the blood of everybody, including the wood-cock, tingled in his veins. The Squire did his best, but cocks are wily ; with a twist round one aged holly, and a turn round another, the bird reached the outside shot free, again did Jack have his chance, but the crisis was too trying for a young sportsman, and a clean miss was the result.

By this time, the Squire, with one barrel left, had run hurriedly to a gap, through which he saw the object of his hopes making a bee line for the big coverts ; in desperation, the Squire threw up his gun, and pulled the trigger; there was a stagger in the steady flight, a second only of further effort, and the bonnie bird, a moment before instinct with life and strength, fell gently on the turf.

" A grand zhot, zir," said Doggett, "seventy yards if 'tis a inch."

"Pick him up," said the Squire, who now felt still less anxiety about the Chudbury bag, and they settled to luncheon withthe appetites of men who had thoroughly done their duty.

BLACKNECKED PHEASANT.

Pheasants Were In Abundance

94

George Doggett -- Gamekeeper

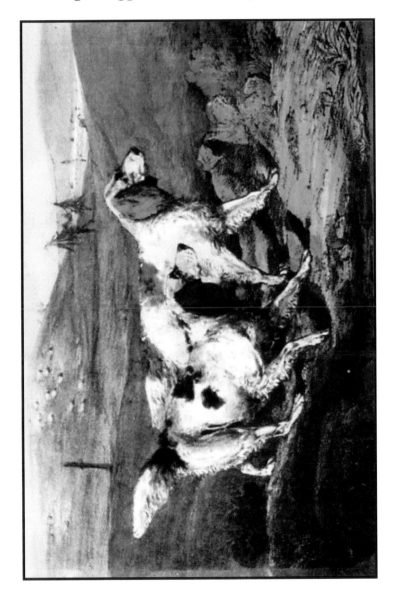

Hunting For Game

95

The remainder of the bag, as originally planned, presented no difficulties, for within an hour after luncheon, two brace of partridges, three pheasants, four couple of rabbits, and a hare, completed the tale, winding up with a wood-pigeon or queest, and two lapwings, as they walked home ; and thus ended one of the most enjoyable days the Squire said he had ever had.

In this view Jack fully concurred, and at the next magistrates' meeting, Mr. Colyton was forced to confess that " the Chudbury bag wasn't in it."

8

DOGGETT'S RESOLVE.

The Hare -- Difficult to Hit
After Thorburn

CHAPTER VIII.

DOGGETT'S RESOLVE.

THE Squire's hints to the Doctor were by no means thrown away, for whilst the patient recovered strength and cheerfulness, and might be considered fairly convalescent, his powers of locomotion by no means improved in the same ratio. At first the interest in the case—as a case—attracted the Doctor, for no one could have received more anxious medical care than Will Murrill; then, as under the influence of sympathy and kindness, the man's natural self reappeared, special attention gave way to general interest, and the Doctor often enjoyed a chat with his patient, who was an intelligent man, and had seen the world. So it was, when suspicion became a certainty, and the permanent nature of Will's lameness could no longer be disguised, it became a painful necessity to announce to the poor fellow what all felt would be a crushing blow; still, longer delay could scarcely be justified in the face of the Squire's strongly expressed wishes, and the Doctor made up his mind to definitely inform Will of his fears for his future.

How did Doggett, all this time, bear the disruption of his home ? I do not believe that he was ever happier, for though reserved, he was affectionate, and having run Will nearly to death, and then saved him at the risk of his own life, he felt a warmth of friendship that no personal discomfort could displace ; so it came about that Doggett was present when the Doctor announced to Will kindly, though without circumlocution, that he would be "crippled for life."

Poor Will ! With a white, startled face, and a shudder— as the real meaning of the Doctor's words came home to him—he could only look from the face of him who pronounced his doom to that of Doggett with eyes of piteous entreaty. To such a man, if the power to wander over the green fields in the fresh air of heaven was taken from him, and the gifts which are given to the poorest, of health and strength, of the power to work and earn his daily bread, were lost, what was left ? Nothing : a life of desolation— a life without hope; do we say a life? No ; a death—a living death; for Will well knew what measure he—friend-less, penniless, and an outcast—would receive from that world whose opinion he had so often braved. Was it, then, a wonder that, with an exceeding bitter cry, he should turn his face to the wall ?

As the Doctor passed out of the cottage, after performing this unpleasant duty, he was accompanied by Doggett, who, as far as his feelings went, was in hardly better state than Will Murrill. On the thresh-

The Doctor Attending

old they paused, and the Doctor, not unkindly, but as stating an obvious fact, said, "There's nothing before him but the workhouse !"

For a moment Doggett looked blankly at the speaker, as though not quite comprehending the meaning of his words, and then, as their full significance burst upon him, his face flushed, and a light shone in his eyes, as he said, simply, " I be on'y a poor man, zir, but, thank God, I got my health an' a pair o' strong arms, an zo long as I a' got they, that poor veller don't go to no workhouse." "But, bless me," said the startled Doctor, "what do you mean to do ? " "I do mean to keep he along o' I, zo long as e's ill," said Doggett, " an' nobody shan't part us, an' I'll tell 'e somethin' more : 'e could a' killed I as easy as easy when I were in that ditch, an' d'you think I be goin' to let un die in a workhouse after savin' un from river ?"

By this time Doggett had worked himself up and run himself down, and as the Doctor had nothing more to say, they parted ; the one rode off, feeling that human nature—as exemplified in Doggett—possessed higher capabilities than he had given it credit for ; the other, with a generous warmth at his heart, re-entered the lodge, and found poor Will completely broken down, having heard the Doctor's suggestion of the workhouse. "Oh, Jarge !" he cried, "to think o' living in they awful places, vour brick walls an a iron pump, never to go out, an to die a pauper!"

Then and there George Doggett sat him down, and tenderly taking the sick man's hand, soothed him, comforted him, and swore to be a brother to him, so that as long as they both should live, he George Doggett did solemnly charge himself with the care of Will Murrill, and Will Murrill believed him; and from that day a tenderness and affection sprang up between the two men, born of sympathy and desire to help on the one side, and simple faith and reliance on the other. But what did Westcombe say to this extraordinary subversion of the proper order of things ?

The Vicar hurried down, post haste, to argue Doggett out of his "absurd infatuation," and after spending a futile half hour, said, " Well, George, you are a foolish fellow to take this burthen upon you, but I honour you," and gave him a sovereign for Will.

When the Squire heard of it he was much annoyed, but didn't believe it! Firstly, he was sure Doggett couldn't be such a fool. Secondly, Doggett had had love passages with a village maiden; and the Squire knew the sex well.

Thirdly, he (the Squire) had not the slightest intention of permitting such Quixotic proceedings; so, sending for Doggett, he plunged at once into the matter with, " George, they tell me you are going to keep that poaching vagabond?"   This was the one interview Doggett dreaded ; he loved the Squire, and knowing that he had no valid reason to influence him, felt very doubtful how it would terminate; but, screwing up his courage, he replied, "If I may make zo bold, zir, I'd like to zay a few words."

" Go on," said the Squire. " You zee, zir," said Doggett, "this poor veller's goin' to be a cripple for life," "Serve him right," said the Squire, "he shouldn't steal my birds," "Nozir, he zees that," said Doggett deprecatingly, "but, zir," he han't got a vriend in the world, an' he han't got a penny piece, 'ceptin what Vicar gaved un, an' 'e must go to th' Union—an' he could a knocked I on the head like a rabbut whilst I were in thic' ditch": this was a strong point with Doggett, and brought out on all occasions some knowledge of the Squire's ways. But it was a sorrowful day for the two men when Doggett returned and recounted his failure. Will only said " Thanky, Jarge, thanky, you've been a good vriend, an' I do like 'e too well to ruin 'e, zo please God I'll go to Union t'morrow,—an' Jarge, you'll come an' zee I sometimes?" he pleadingly added.

This was too much for George, who again solemnly pledged himself that Will never should go to the Union, but nevertheless it was with heavy hearts that the two men speculated on the chances of the Squire's giving way, for otherwise they could see no way out of the coil.

" Zo, zir, as a man, I couldn't, after pullin' un out o' river, I couldn't let un go, I couldn't rely, an' I do hope you'll let un stay."

There was such a world of piteous entreaty in the keeper's face, that recounting the interview afterwards to Mrs. Wynheard, the Squire was forced to confess that if he had not set his heart like a flint, he would have been as big a fool as Doggett, but he gave the keeper fully to understand that Will should go, and that quickly. It must not be supposed that the females of Westcombe intended to be left out in this matter ; some applauded, others derided, but Doggett had a strong ally in Mrs. Wynheard, who had gone down many a time to see Will at the lodge, and was both interested in his future and wished him well.

On hearing of Doggett's resolve, Mrs. Wynheard gave them both to understand, that although she could not vouch for the Squire, she considered Doggett a hero, and bade them be of good cheer, as "things" would in the end turn out all right. It was the remembrance of this cheering prophecy on the part of Mrs. Wynheard that imparted some rays of light into the darkness which at this time encompassed Will's prospects, and although there was an absence of definition in the " things" which were " to turn out all right," yet

Doggett shrewdly credited Mrs. Wynheard with great influence brought out on all occasions some knowledge of the Squire's ways. But it was a sorrowful day for the two men when Doggett returned and recounted his failure. Will only said "Thanky, Jarge, thanky, you've been a good vriend, an' I do like 'e too well to ruin 'e, zo please God I'll go to Union t'morrow,—an' Jarge, you'll come an' zee I sometimes?" he pleadingly added.

This was too much for George, who again solemnly pledged himself that Will never should go to the Union, but nevertheless it was with heavy hearts that the two men speculated on the chances of the Squire's giving way, for otherwise they could see no way out of the coil.

Where was little Jack all this time ? He was running in and out of the Lodge, and although he never swerved in his allegiance to Doggett, his heart had gone out to Will, for Will could make such whistles ; Will could make fishing rods and bats and traps of all sorts, and cunning carvings when he grew better. On the afternoon of this eventful day Jack appeared as usual, and then and there did Doggett unburden his load of woe to the sympathising little lad.

With tears streaming down his cheeks, he rushed breathlessly to the Hall ; there he found the Squire, and said between his sobs, "Oh father ! dear

Will Would Miss the Rural Scenes

father ! please let Will stay ; it'll break George's heart if he goes, and you promised me a new pony, and I don't want one if only you'll let Will stay, and he can have my half-crown if he hasn't any money, can't he, father dear ?"

" Bless the lad," said the squire huskily. " There, run along and tell George, if he will be a fool he must, and Murrill can stay and help feed the pheasants." It did not take long for Jack to find his way back to the Lodge with the glad tidings, and that night a great peace and content reigned, not only in the hearts of Doggett and Will but at the Hall, and Mrs Wynheard, when her husband told her what he had done, only said, "Thank you, John".

9

PHOEBE FITTON

SPEAKS HER MIND.

Phoebe and a Friend

CHAPTER IX

PHOEBE FITTON

SPEAKS HER MIND.

It was well understood in the village that George Doggett had made up his mind, and when George Doggett had arrived at that point, you could as easily turn Niagara. Like many men who live comparatively lonely lives, he thought long before committing himself to a line of action which once taken was, in his view, almost irrevocable.

Sunday after Sunday—weather permitting—the keeper's footsteps would wander towards the end of the village, where, enshrined in a one-story casket, with a thatch top, was the jewel which hitherto had attracted honest George.

Many a girl in Westcombe set her cap at our friend, for he was the most eligible amongst the bachelors; but year after year he piloted his skiff amongst these rocks and shoals, heedless of the sirens, whose designs were, to tell the truth, very palpable ; but, at last, through sheer force of circumstances, George had

The Forge
Home of the Fittons

succumbed to the charms of Phoebe Fitton.

For many a year the Fittons had lived at Westcombe Forge—the founder of the family having shoed the horses of the Squire's grandfather. The present master of the house kept up his grandsire's reputation for honest work, and was as lusty a son of Vulcan as you could wish to see. The little forge itself had always its knot of loungers, and it may well be believed by those who know village ways, that the operations of the forge were unaccompanied by any symptom of indecent haste, and that the circulation of country gossip was uncommonly brisk round the anvil. The daughter of the house, christened Phoebe, was a buxom lass, and—it must be confessed— knew it; she was also a flirt—a village flirt—and had had soft passages with a certain Tom Trip, believing it wise to follow the proverb of "double strings," and judiciously manipulating Thomas against George, and George against Thomas.

Still, certain it was, that in due course, "all things being equal," Phoebe Fitton would mind such a feeling of wrath as was likely to give George Doggett, when he made his next visit, a very unpleasant quarter of an hour.

It was hard, too, for Phoebe to receive the condolences of her female friends, framed with a specious smoothness the very acme of feminine spite, for no sooner was George's decision known in reference to

Will, than the relations between Phoebe and himself were discussed, and it was not as oil on the troubled waters of the girl's pride for Patty Snow—a rival for the affections of Doggett—to observe, "Jarge Doggett become Mrs. George Doggett, and mistress of the Lodge—a destiny for which she conceived herself 've got a housemaid, I'd' hear, Phoebe, a' won't want to put up 'they askins yet a bit." Nor did it help to make the position more supportable to hear — of eminently suited. But are the fates ever kind ? Here, with the prize almost in her grasp—for George, though, according to village customs, her accepted suitor, was not so pledged but that he might, without loss of honour, withdraw his head from the matrimonial noose—arose an impediment, not a lawful, just one, but " a low poarching veller," as Phoebe expressed it to her mother, arousing in her (Phoebe's) course, accidentally—that Tom Trip had been seen walking out with a Chudbury girl on two successive evenings. The position then being strained, it cannot be wondered at that Phoebe determined to have it out with George on the next Sunday afternoon.

I do not think it ever occurred to George that he was behaving unfairly to Phoebe, although it was manifestly the case; but sure it is, he did not go Fittonwards with his usual alacrity, and as he drew near the cottage certain misgivings passed through his mind whether Phoebe—as a girl of spirit—would quietly acquiesce in any arrangement that he proposed to suggest.

Phoebe was in the garden, and having watched her lover down the road for the last quarter of a mile, was prepared to respond to his " Well, Phoebe !" with a start of well-assumed surprise and a "La, Jarge !

How you did vrighten me." Here the conversation languished, for, after the manner of village swains. Doggett was " slow of invention," and "not cunning of speech." A pause of considerable length was broken by the remark, "Pointer pup 've broke 's leg."

A warm expression of sympathy from Phoebe in the accident to the luckless pup, and again the portals closed, the keeper being, "It fairly gravelled for want of matter." But by this time they were both aware of a "something" stretching its malign influence across the conversational horizon ; yet once again did George, by a happy inspiration, evolve a series of questions concerning the physical well being of the Fitton family, commencing with, " How's your vather ?" and going down to little Benjy, its minutest, eighth member ; but even they came to an end, and at last, driven to desperation, he plunged into the matter which was occupying both their minds, with " Will Murrill don't zim to get much better.

Doctor zays he'll be crippled vor life." No sympathetic response from Phoebe. " He told I," continued Doggett, " he'd have to go into th' House."

Again he stopped, but seeing a gathering sparkle in Phoebe's eyes, certainly not sympathetic, hurried on in anticipation of the coming storm. " But there, I've made up my mind he shan't go in to no House, vor 'tis a cruel thing, a barbareous act, to put such a man as he in the House, zo I told un 'e could stay wi' I till zo be as 'e's better, an' Zquire zays he can, tho' 'e wor mighty vext to virst, till Master Jack got un round."

Here George stopped and wiped his face, down which a perspiration of mingled emotions was pouring. Then did Phoebe Fitton discharge the full vials of her wrath on the luckless head of Doggett. " I've heard tell of many vools i' my time, George Doggett, but there's vools and vools, an' if zo be you like to keep a low poarching-veller, an' look after un an' spend your money on encouragin' zuch as he, tho' how Zquire do let 'e do ut's a wonder t' I,—'taint vor me t ' enquire, but there's them as knows what comfort's like, an' what 'tis to have zome one to make 'em comfortable and cook their vittles, an' mend their things tidy-like, an' zo," said Phoebe, being by this time run down and desirous of making a dignified retreat, " you'm go your way, an I'm go mine, an' I wish 'e well wi' yoar poarcher." With this Parthian shaft, Phoebe retired, defeated but not disgraced , vowing " he should come there no more."

At the same time her thrifty, housewifely heart saddened at the thought of the loss of the rabbits and hares which had been the *gages d'amours* from the keeper to his love.

As to George, he retired with mixed feelings ; no man likes to be called a " vool," more particularly when he thinks perhaps he is one, but underlying this, came the ever comforting reflection that it was over so Will and he would not be separated or interfered with now, and things would come right somehow.

Then he set to work to justify the course he had taken by bringing Will's good points to the front, and praising him wherever and whenever he got the chance. Truly, Will was a handyman, in every sense of the word ; as he grew stronger, things righted them-selves as if by magic under his fingers: pheasants that would not lay and hens that refused to sit were nursed to a sense of their duties, and families of feathered bi-peds, with strength and feather never before known at Westcombe, clucked and cheeped and cackled and scratched round the breeding hutches; old clocks that had stopped for years, rejoiced the hearts of their owners by brightened faces and correct time—gates were mended—cracked panes replaced—stubborn locks closed sweetly, and as if it was once again a plea-sure to them to be locked.

And the Lodge ! No mansion was neater nor brighter; racks of quaint designs — Will's carving— held the guns; and shelves, and bits of homely, but useful furniture, gradually appeared, till the Lodge was the best furnished house in the village. Will was never idle, but became a necessity to Westcombe, and gradually won the esteem and good-will of the district by his unfailing cheerfulness and ready help; as is often the case, Will's sins once condoned, he became a favourite amongst his betters, the Squire confessing him to be a useful man about the place, whilst the Vicar said he possessed "an unusual intelligence."

Now this favourable verdict was due to the fact that the Vicar, being an enthusiastic angler, very soon discovered that Will was no mean performer with the rod, and above all things, was an "up stream fisher," certain it is, that the only time the worthy man ever was known to lose his temper was on the question of " up stream," versus " down stream " fishing, and as Will's view coincided with the Vicar's on this important point, and the Vicar loved a companion—that is to say an appreciative one—Will's recovery was anticipated with some impatience, in order that the pools and stickles of the neighbouring river might be despoiled.

Will Was A Useful Fishing Companion

Fishing for Trout

10

THE

BIG TROUT.

Trout in the River

CHAPTER X.

T H E BIG TROUT

AN April morning ! A morning- of smiles and tears, gentle showers and bright sunshine, a morning of bursting buds, and humming insects, a morning of rising trout, of trout pining to be basketed, a day whose claim on anglers was so obtrusive that the Vicar yielded a willing ear to the seductive tongue of Will Murrill, when he hobbled up to the Vicarage with the news that there was a wonderful show of duns on the water, and the fish rising all over the place.

Strict regard for truth compels me to state that Will Murrill's persuasions had an ample backing in the Vicar's inclinations, for a careful survey of his barometer, the way of the wind, and general indications, had given him an acute attack of " fishing fever," of which he was a constant, though willing victim. Nine o'clock on this beautiful fishing morning found the Vicar and Will in anxious conclave over the probabilities of the sport ; for be it known that, to your "regular angler,"

the delights of preparation are by no means an insig-
nificant item in the pleasures of the day ; the casts
arranged, the knotty question of red spinner and pale
blue versus March brown and April dun being decided
in favour of casts of each, and a nice luncheon—for the
Vicar believed in creature comforts—packed in a basket, they started for the river.

Surely the man is much to be pitied who knows
not of the delights of angling. Angling does not mean
the mere catching of fish ; it is beyond this, it opens
artistic possibilities, a world of ever changing delights
to the watchful eye and heedful ear, a world which is
closed to those who use not the opportunities of which
almost all men can take advantage. Volumes can be
written of the beasts, birds, insects, and flowers, found
on the banks of our rivers, of their ways and habits, of
their growth, of the fragrance of the trees and flowers.

With what pleasure do we note the streamlets,
with a wreath of colour lining their banks ; crimson
ragged Robin, hob nobbing with white Starwor; pale
Primrose and golden Buttercup side by side; Violets
blue and Violets white perfuming the air yard by yard
; Ivy and Periwinkle wandering idly hand-in-hand ;
and the stream itself, so daintily fringed with grasses,
and blue Forget-me-nots, which sway this way and
that, anon kissing the little rills as they ripple laughingly past, then waving their adieux to the bubbles as
they hurry onward, ever onward, and twinkling their

Kingfisher

Sand Martens

Adult: Right

Young: Left:

Under the banks are nests innumerable, Sand-
Martens and Kingfishers, Throstles and Ouzels.

golden eyes as they bend saucily to speed them on their way. Then the river itself —the beauty of water in rapid movement has a fascination all its own—the ripple, ripple, ripple, and the occasional splash, the rush as it passes through a narrow gorge, and the sullen plunge as it falls into the silent pool, are all and each perfect in their way. The life, too, of the river is more pronounced than that of the streamlet: the banks are less brightly colored, but here it is that the Hart's-tongue, the Ladyfern, and lordly Burdock love to dwell; here, too, crouches the timid hare, and idly wanders the painted pheasant, whilst coiled on a bare and sunny spot basking lies " ye spotted snake."

Under the banks are nests innumerable, Sand-Martens and Kingfishers, Throstles and Ouzels, whilst Swallows skim the surface of the water, picking here a fly and there a fly. A sharp tweat, tweat, as a line of brilliant scarlet and blue flashes past, and with the hurry of a "Queen's messenger, a Kingfisher has gone up stream, whilst flop into the water—just at your favourite pool—drops a solemn old water rat, who has been nibbling roots, and watching you with a wary eye as you work up stream. Oh ! that I had the pen of a Moore, for then would I write me a poem on the "Loves of the Ouzels."   For the perfection of bird courtship, give me the fascinating ways of a pair of ouzels : there they are, chattering and twittering on a stone in the stream, their snowy throats doubly white by contrast with their dusky bodies. The male—encouraging, persuasive, adoring; the female—shy, modest, but enticing. Then in pure gladness of heart does he spread his wings, soaring up for a few yards singing, as though to burst his little throat, a perfect pean ; whilst she, flirts her tail, and ducks her little head, as though to say, "Do it again, please." ***All this—and much more—does the angler notice instinctively, whilst he watches for the " bell" or " rise" of a big fish.***

At last, at the head of a stream, above a jutting stone, comes the welcome signal. These natural beauties were not thrown away upon the Vicar and Will, for both were ardent lovers of Nature ; but, having thus far digressed from sheer supra-abundance of material, we will now return to the more prosaic point of filling our baskets.

Will's lameness interfered little with his angling powers, for what he lacked in agility he made up in skill, and he could, when walking with the Vicar, potter along sufficiently quickly as pool after pool, and stickle after stickle was fished. Certainly the day was propitious, and the Vicar an artist, for the point fly dropped here and searched there with a deftness which aroused Will's admiration. "Yo drows a beautiful vly, zir," said Will. " I do mind only one genleman as ever I zeed as drowd zo good a line ' twer years ago, an' 'e told I all I d'know, vor I a' carried 's basket many

a time. He always drowed up stream 'ceptin' zome-
times, an' then he'd drow a dry vly ; wonderful 'twas
to zee un cast."

Then the Vicar would come out, and discuss
the question of dry fly versus sunk ditto, until he saw
a good fish rise; then would he quietly cast over him,
and generally capture the too-confiding victim. The
basket grew heavy apace, for the fish rose as if they
meant it; no coming short, but a good honest snatch at
the fly, a gleam in the water, an almost imperceptible
movement of the angler's wrist, a tightened line, bent
rod, and the 'struggle commenced,

They had gradually worked their way up stream,
till they came to a point where the river winding round
a bend was deep with a strong current.

" Ah !" said the Vicar regretfully, " this was the
place where I hooked the largest fish I ever saw in
the Axe, and he broke me, broke me fairly, just under that bank. I had him on nearly five minutes, and
thought I was sure of him, but in his last rush he carried everything away. Perhaps I was just a little too
quick." "Maybe he's there yet," said Will. The words
had hardly left his lips, when at a point corresponding
with the Vicar's description, was seen the bell of a large
fish. " I believe that's the very fellow," said the Vicar
excitedly. " Now, zir," said Will, "you take off your drop-
per an' ony use your point vly, an' just put it over 'e
nicely." All this the Vicar did *secundem artem,* but

the fish rose again and again at the natural, without looking at the artificial fly; about his size there was no doubt—he was a grand fish, and worth any amount of trouble. " I'd come out, zir, ef I was you, an' give un a rest like," said Will, as the Vicar kept casting again and again.

Seeing the propriety of the suggestion, the Vicar reluctantly retreated to the bank. "Now, zir," said Will, "the way to catch e's to giv un a dry vly, an' vioat it down to un, vor a won't have they zunk zpiders nohow." Here was a pill for the Vicar: all his life had he fished up stream with spiders, allowing them to sink, but now he was beaten, the fish would have none of him ; so, like a wise man, he put his prejudices in his pocket, and his fly on the cast, and carefully creeping opposite the still rising fish, sent a floating dun deftly some two feet above the monster. This time there was neither hesitation nor disdain ; leisurely sucking it in as it floated down, the great yellow fellow rolled complacently over, till, feeling the tightening of the line, he suspected something wrong, and with a rush, which tried every knot in the cast, and sent the line whizzing through the rings, he made for his hover ; it was no use attempting to stop him, for the casting line was a fine one, and the Vicar could only hope that neither rock nor root was likely to break it.

Reeling up as the fish stopped, the battle began : the water was deep, and the fish knew his whereabouts, and meant to stay there, but the stream was strong, and as the strain on the rod told, he made a gallant rush for freedom and life. Down he went, right away, faster than the Vicar could follow, for the banks were awkward ; as yard after yard of line was run off, the Vicar did his best, and at last succeeded in coming opposite the fish, which by this time had run into a mass of waving green weed, out of which he had no mind to budge, but boring in deeper and deeper as the Vicar got more and more desperate, it seemed any odds on the fish.

Again Will's advice was valuable, " You'm go in, zir, an' poke he out wi' handle o' your landing net, an' I'll hold the rod an' let un run ef so be a do come out." Seeing nothing else for it, if he wished to save the fish, the Vicar consented, and boldly entering the stream, worked his way towards the fish, unmindful of prospective rheumatism from a cold trickle down his legs as the water slowly rose over the edge of his waders ; as he probed the weed, the occupant finding the butt end of the landing net in dangerous proximity to his nose, hurried out for pastures new, but he had no longer the command of locality—he was flurried, and by the time the Vicar gained the bank and took the rod in hand, the fish was spent, and might be landed at the next shallow.

There he made one more effort—a valiant one—but weakened by the protracted struggle, it was the last. Slowly the reel was wound up, and the yellow sides came into view, as the spotted beauty feebly protested against the indignity of his capture.

" Four pounds if he's an ounce," said the delighted Vicar, deftly sliding the net under and lifting him up to the admiring gaze of Will. When, *o tempora ! o mores*! the net, an old one and rotten, broke at the bottom, and with a splash, the great trout fell souse into the water, breaking the casting line in his fall.

" Confound the net," said the disgusted clergyman, surprised by this appalling catastrophe out of all ecclesiastical propriety, " I shall never hook such a fish again." " Dear, dear," said Will, with a gasp of dismay, " who'd a thought ut ? " " And the worst of it is," said the Vicar, "I've gone in over my waders, and am wet to the skin."

Very dejectedly they sauntered home, bewailing their loss, but gradually raising the weight of the losttrout, until by the time the Vicarage was reached, it had become a full five pounds and more. Never again did the Vicar behold that big trout. Whether a ripe experience led him to eschew flies, or whether the casting line was too much for a digestion enfeebled by this momentous struggle, no one will ever know; but sure it is that to this day the Vicar tells the tale of how he lost, but nearly basketed, *"The Big Trout.".*

11

JACK GOES
TO SCHOOL.

Jack Was to Become a Fine Young Man

CHAPTER XI.

JACK GOES TO SCHOOL.

SOME time having elapsed since Will Murrill became an inmate of the Lodge, and Jack's education having been carried forward to a point at which the Vicar thought he might with advantage to his pupil transfer it to other hands, the question was discussed between the Squire and himself as to the benefit to be obtained from sending the boy to a public school. Here the Vicar's views were decided. " Your lad must go from home to gain independence of mind, and find his level, and if I am any judge," continued he, "his level should be a high one; apart from that, his playfellows at present are villagers, and it will be well for him to live amongst others of his own rank, and make school friendships which may last him all his life."

In this the Squire concurred, but it was a terrible wrench, for the l ittle lad had become his ally so it was hard to part from his boy just when he was becoming a companion and friend, the single-hearted affection between the two being more that of brothers than father and son. The sting of the separation was somewhat lessened to the Squire by his wife presenting him—to the astonishment of the neighbourhood—with a second boy, whom they decided to call Geoffrey after Sir Geoffrey de Wynheard, the founder of the name, and the original of the remarkable portrait in stone which adorned the walls of the Squire's pew, and caused so much speculation in Jack's mind.

To Jack, although dearly loving his father, the excitement of the preparation for school was sufficient to moderate his grief, and except for a few tears which he shed on leaving his mother, and a huskiness which pervaded the voices of both father and son when the Squire left him, he bore up bravely.

The Squire's parting was characteristic, and conveyed somewhat in these words," Now, Jack, your mother and I want to be proud of you ; never forget what she's taught you, never tell a lie, and own up at once if you get into trouble, never hurt a boy smaller than yourself, never seek a fight, but if it is forced on you remember to fight as long as you can stand for the

Jack Excelled at Cricket

honour of Westcombe. God Bless You."

The parting between Jack, George Doggett, and Will was a serious matter. The necessity of sending Jack away to school could not be brought home to George and Will, but as they both agreed, " Master Jack do know a deal more'n we, an he can zhut a rabbut, an vor the matter o' that a znipe zo well as I," said George ; "an a neater drower wi a vly I never zeed," attested Will; " but there, Jarge, we'm not let un zee as we do care zo ter-rible much, or p'raps a' won't go, an Zquire'll be angry." So George and Will agreed to take a cheerful view of mat-ters, to keep special eyes on all his pets, and make elabo-rate preparations in the way of ferrets, and rods, traps, and flies, against his home coming.

It is not our intention to closely follow his school life ; he proved the sagaciousness of the Vicar's forecast by becoming a popular boy and a power in the school, and, thanks to his mother's teaching, the power was exercised for good. He followed out his father's advice by seldom fighting, but when he did, he fought for the honour of Westcombe.

Jack Wynheard was a boy to be remembered, and in the school traditions are many records of what he did, and how he did it. His Homeric combats, whereof the history of one survives to this day and is handed down as such an one as the heroes of old loved and fought : his climb to the top of the big fir, which had baffled successive generations of boys : and his great innings, when, with everything apparently against his school, he went in third wicket down, and carrying out his bat converted what appeared about to be a disas- trous defeat into a brilliant victory : all these and more, are they not written in the memories of old boys, and treasured up by the Squire, the Vicar, the Doctor, and Doggett, and Will, to whom the Squire imparted such bits of school news as he knew would give them pleasure.

But time passed, and passed with the giant strides he makes for the old, and the lagging footsteps that halt for the young.

Jack left school for a military tutor, as nothing would satisfy the lad but a soldier's career. His heart was so set upon it that even his mother gave a reluc- tant consent, whilst the Squire had visions of seeing once again a line of " fighting Wynheards," of whom both the noseless crusader and the ancestor who, barely escaped hanging in Monmouth's time were notable examples.

In due course Jack was gazetted to a dragoon regiment, and great there at was the excitement and demoralisation at Westcombe, for when it became known that "th' young Squire," as he was now called, was a dragoon—a real "sojer"—visions of scarlet and gold, ribbons and trumpets, so inflamed tile youth of Westcombe, that three or four then and there enlisted, of whom all repented, and were bought off next day, save one, a fine young fellow, named Mat Weston, who, with the unanimous approval of the village, became Jack's servant and humble friend.

All this time little Geoff was growing bravely, and doing his best to fill the void left by Jack's departure; he had become as indispensable to his father as Jack had been, and although nothing could alter the affection of Doggett and Will for the older brother, there was a corner into which Geoff had managed to squeeze himself.

The affection, too, between the brothers was very pleasant to witness, Geoff worshipping Jack as only a little boy can, and the elder returning the hero worship with an interest very real and lovable.

12

HOW THE V.C. CAME TO WESTCOMBE.

The Victoria Cross

CHAPTER XII.
HOW THE V.C. CAME TO WESTCOMBE.

AS a heavy dragoon, popular Jack Wynheard was a success. Just six feet high in his stockings; with a thoroughly well-knit frame inured to every athletic exercise, and, with a frank open countenance, he presented as as the eye often rests upon; add to this, that under Doggett's tuition, his shooting was well-nigh perfection; that he rode fearlessly and well; and Jack Wynheard may be held to have begun life under favourable auspices.

He worked hard at his profession, for, like the Squire, he was very thorough, yet found time for many a run down to Westcombe, where his advent was ever hailed by every one on the estate. But there was destined to be a rude awakening from this pleasant dream of life : bad news came from the Crimea, then worse, and before long Jack's regiment was ordered on foreign service.

It was a sorrowful leave-taking, but all the village of Westcombe felt that the occasion was one for congratulation for the allied armies, and that the sword of the young Squire was destined to cut a road to fortune for himself, and honour for his country.

With an air of mystery, the Squire on the last day of his stay took his son to the stables, and with gratified pride presented him with a horse—such a horse !! For a full five minutes Jack could do nothing but walk round him, whilst the delighted Squire showed his points. Bucket, the old groom, endorsed the Squire's encomiums with " zo 'tis, zir, an he 'm better'n 'e do look," and " they'm never catch ee, Muster Jack, if zo be you be a top o' 'e;" the primary duty of a dragoon being, in Bucket's eyes, to take care of his skin, and keep well out of the way. In the evening came Doggett, and presenting his humble duty, hoped Mr. Jack would accept "a bit of a box" from Will and him, which Jack did with great delight, the said box being a quaint old silver tobacco-box, with a motto and initials on the lid. The history of this box was as follows :—It was borne in upon Will that Doggett and he ought, at this critical period of the young Squire's life, to give him a special memento.

Doggett agreed, and Will went to Axminster on a voyage of discovery; there he found the " tobacco box" above mentioned, and as he explained to Doggett, " Master Jack may often want a bit o bacca'

144

The Squire's Gift to Jack

an then he'll think o we, zo to make zure I told zhopkeeper to put young zquire's name a top, an' at bottom I told un to put-- Wen this you zee Remember we. G.D , W.M, G.D. that's you; W.M, that's me; and a heart wi a arrer thro' un," which being copied from a valentine that Will had seen some twenty years before, and the sweet appropriateness of which had made a deep impression on his mind,could scarcely be termed original; and yet was loyally accepted as such by George.

At first the Squire received letters with some regularity, but as the regiment moved further and further, he was obliged to rest content with newspaper reports, and privileged communications from special correspondents. I do not think that it entered the minds of any Westcombe folk that serious danger could surround the young Squire, so the shock of a despatch from the War Office, curtly announcing Cornet Wynheard wounded, was like an earthquake.

Within an hour the Squire was at the station on his way to London to gain full information, whilst the Vicar wandered about in a partly demented fashion, reviling war generally; and Doggett and Will, whom the news had reached, thought it no shame to their manhood to let the tears trickle down their cheeks as they wondered "if powder were bad, as young Zquire never missed wi's fust barrel an generally killed wi's second."

At the War Office a friendly under-secretary, with whom the Squire was "well acquent," gave him further particulars, comprised in a short despatch just come in—"Sharp skirmish, near ....Killed, Captain Sandys ; badly wounded, Sergeant Bates, Troopers Smith, Follows, Weston; slightly wounded, Cornet Wynheard." . With this the poor Squire was obliged to be content, and with a promise from the under-secretary that the next information received should be forwarded to him without delay, the Squire returned to Westcombe.

There he was besieged—half the adjoining counties seemed roused at the knowledge of his son's danger, and the enquiries were endless. During this time of terrible anxiety nothing gave the Squire so much relief as the warm and ready sympathy of Doggett and Will, and he would, day after day, go down to chat at the Lodge.

" 'Tis killin Zquire, I do b'lieve," said Doggett, one day to Will, " he'm years older."

Just at that moment they espied the Squire, with a newspaper in his hand, striding down the drive towards the cottage, at something approaching five miles an hour—"Zquire've got news, an good news too, I'll be bound," said Doggett. "Tis zure," said Will, "he'm like a vour year old." Just then the Squire, with a face radiant as a sunbeam, entered the door with, " Good news, Doggett ! Capital news !"

" Thank God," said Will piously. "Yes!" replied the Squire reverently, and then, "listen to this:" "From our Special Correspondent," "that's a fellow who goes with the army and looks after these things," explained the Squire. " Like a earth-stopper," suggested Doggett " Yes, yes, just so," replied the Squire, and continuing—"A very gallant thing was done in the last skirmish. Cornet Wynheard, of the ——th Dragoons, saw a wounded trooper helping an 82nd man ; the enemy were pressing close, Wynheard turned back as the trooper's horse fell; there was time to put the wounded man on the officer's horse and send him on, when the enemy were upon them. Wynheard shot three." " I know'd it," burst in Doggett triumphantly. "I told Will I wer zure e'd get 's right an left, an maybe three out o' a covey—if they crossed," said Doggett hastily, for he remembered the Squire's dislike to firing into the brown*. " Wait a bit," said the Squire ; " shot three and cut down two as they rushed on; unfortunately the 82nd man was struck down, and before our fellows came up and brought them in, Wynheard got a nasty cut.

The General has sent in his name for the V. C., and never was it more richly deserved. There !! " said the delighted Squire, " what do you think of that? The Victoria Cross for valour in the field !"— and

* Expression used when a covey is fired into without taking aim, whereby many birds'are wounded, few killed.

148

leaving Doggett and Will almost besides themselves with pride and delight—strode hastily away to intercept the Vicar, and anyone else whom he could find.

Of course Jack's gallantry was the talk of the country side, and as all who knew him loved him, the congratulations which poured in upon the beatified Squire were real and hearty. In due course, two letters were received -- one from Mat Weston, telling how Jack had saved his life at the risk of his own, and how the regiment one and all swore there never was such an officer; the other from Jack, in which he expressed his delight at his V. C. ; still more at his being invalided home, and containing a special message to Doggett and Will, that the "bacca- box" had saved his life by stopping a nasty thrust, which otherwise would have astonished his vitals, for so vicious was the stab that it cut the silver through, obliterating the "heart and arrer."

Salmon -- The Fisherman's Dream

13

HIS FIRST SALMON.

Salmon & Trout

CHAPTER XIII.

HIS FIRST SALMON.

A DULL October morning found Geoff wandering aim-lessly around the Hall, divided in mind whether he should take Vie and Di—his faithful terriers—for a day's rabbiting, or inveigle Doggett into a walk round the outlying doubles, in the hope of finding a peripatetic pheasant, whom black- berries and dropping acorns had seduced from the sheltering corners of the Holrnwood.

Twice had he gone to the stables to while away an hour in interesting debate over the feeding, dress-ing, and capabilities of his pony ; carefully had he ex-amined every rat-trap, in the hope of finding a victim ready to expiate his offences at the fangs of his canine followers, and yet time hung heavy on his hands, for the traps were empty, and the day dull and uninvit-ing. "Whatever shall I do ? " said Geoff for the twenti-eth time; the question was unexpectedly answered by the appearance of Tom Twite, breathless with haste and anxiety, speeding along the drive. Geoff hailed him with, " Halloo ! Tommy, what's up ? " Between native bashfulness and the excitement of being the bearer of

Fishing for Salmon

154

good news, Tommy stuck, twisting his cap and gasping in the intervals of recovering breath, he stammered out, " Will Murrill— have sent I—to tell 'e as there's— a zammon in Withy Pool."

All listlessness disappeared from Geoff's face as if by magic, for if he had an ambition unfulfilled it was to kill a salmon. His chances were very few, for fish could rarely run up the river as far as Westcombe, many and keen being the watchful eyes past which they ran the gauntlet; but here, at last, when, too, he least expected it, came his opportunity. To dash into the house, snatch up a rod and reel of his brother's, slip a fly book into his pocket containing a few old salmon flies—treasured relics—to tear off at fastest pace towards the keeper's lodge was to Geoff only the work of a minute. At his heels followed Tom Twite, fully as excited and wishful to see the sport. A five minutes' run brought them to the Lodge, where Will Murrill, anxiously awaiting them, stood talking to John Fry. " Oh, Will ! " said Geoff, breathlessly, "are you sure ?" Well! Mast'r Geoff," replied Will, " I didn't zee un, but you, Jan, you tell Mast'r Geoff ! " Thus adjured, John Fry related how he was hedging near Withy Pool, when his attention was attracted to the river by a splash in the centre ; he thought it was a otter," but a second and louder splash decided him against that view, whilst a third disturbance, accompanied by the sight of a broad blacktail made John throw down his bill-hook and rush precipitately with the glad tidings to the Lodge. As quickly as possible (due consideration being accorded to Will's lameness), they made their way to the Withy Pool, and in answer to Geoff's anxious enquiries, John Fry related again and again the appearance of the fish, gradually increasing the size of the tail till it attained such enormous proportions that to Geoff's excited imagination a picture was presented of a salmon so prodigious, that to land it required the united strength of all Westcombe, aided and abetted by sundry teams.

In due coarse the river was reached at a point below the Withy Pool, and here Will Murrill became paramount, his knowledge and experience being allowed to be—in that district at least—unique.

" Doan't 'e be in zuch a takin, Master Geoff; vish woan't vly away," was Will's calmative remark to Geoff, who was, as John Fry expressed it, " ditherin like a aspen," and carefully soaking the trace which he observed was too dry, Will quietly hunted over Geoff's fly book with a running comment of " I wouldn't give much for 'e they do call un the 'Doctor,' but a won't doctor no fish hereabouts, nor this un won't do he'm— not right colour." " Try thiccy," said John Fry, captivated by the blazing glory of a "Jock Scott."

" Thiccy i'deed," said Will, " ef zo be I wer a 'ooman an waanted a Zunday bonnet wi zummat zmart, I'd put he in, but this'll do, one as I giv' cap'n 'fore 'a went awaay ; a turkey veather wi' a yaller hackle an' a bit o' gold twist on 's body—he'll do;" and putting the rod together, tenderly remarked, " You got Cap'n's rod, Master Geoff, mind you do use'n well."

The feelings of the excited quartette were roused to a high pitch by the fish again rising in the very place marked by John Fry, and even Murrill's pulses quickened as he passed the line through the rings. After carefully knotting the trace, and fastening on the fly, he said to the impatient boy, " Now you try a drow or two here, Master Geoff, afore you goes vor 'e." After a minute or two spent in practice, Will thought the time had come, and said, " Now, Mast Geoff, go and catch un, but keep well back, vor ef you can zee jzammon, zam'mon can zee 'ee; zo keep well down an get above un, an drow down to un."

Thus admonished, Geoff crept slowly and cautiously up the stream, keeping well back, until he reached a point some distance above the fish, when gaining the side and creeping down the bank, he gradually brought his fly down the pool—a moment of breathless suspense as the turkey feather and gold twist hung for a second a yard or two above the spot where the fish was last seen, then a break in the water, a pull at the fly, and Geoff was fast in his first salmon. I do not think anything can equal the sensation of hooking your first salmon,unless it may be shooting your first tiger on foot; the momentary pause before the grand rush of the fish, the tension of every nerve; eye, and hand, alike alert ; and then the scream of the reel as the Salmon goes on his run of twenty, thirty, or it may be sixty yards, terminating it by springing, a mass of molten silver, three feet into the air.

Geoff's fish behaved in the orthodox manner, in that he made his momentary pause, and then went—ah! how he did go! Whir-'r-'r-'r went the reel, the sweetest music the delighted lad had ever heard, and amidst the cheering of Will Murrill, the shouts of John Fry, the feeble yet ecstatic pipe of Tom Twite, out ran five and twenty yards of line up stream. "Let un go, Mast'r Geoff, don't 'ee stop un, don't 'ee," implored Will, pale with excitement, " or he'll break 'ee zure." " Pull un out, Mast'r Geoff, draw un up th' bank an I'll catch un vor 'ee," yelled John Fry, bill-hook in hand, regardless alike of the rules of fishing, and possibilities of the situation. " Hooray !" piped little Tom.

Fortunately for Geoff 's credit he let the fish run, and under Will's advice, followed as quickly as he could. "Get yer cast out o' water zoon as 'ee can, Master Geoff, pass on always told I to zhorten line, an drownd 'em quick."

The advice was good, but the fish didn't see it, for by the time Geoff had reeled up he was ready for another spin, and this time thirty yards of line paid out. A second time Geoff reeled up, but the fish was immovable.

" He'm zulking,' said Will, "we'm drow in a ztone." Then it was that the patience of the real salmon fisher showed itself; like a log the fish lay, till at last with a rush and a whirl,   which to the excited onlookers appeared like demoniacal possession that salmon made straight for a large root that loomed ominously near the centre of the river. " Now, Master Geoff, we'm turn un afore he do get there, or we'm lose un,' said Will; so, bit by bit, Geoff got on terms with the fish helped by a strong stream in his favour, and within three yards of the fateful root, aided by a well-aimed clod from John Fry, turned him down stream. "Reel up an' keep in zhort, an' we'm land un at stickle, below Withy Pool,' shouts Will.

The salmon now meant steady business, for he had run hard ; that he was a big fish and well-hooked was certain, as he had never shewn himself. A series of short runs brought them to the Withy Pool, below which lay the eventful stickle. By this time,—nearly half-an-hour since the fish had been hooked,—-the first flush of excitement had been succeeded by an anxious calm ; the interest was almost too deep for words.

The Withy Pool was gained and passed, stickle succeeded pool and pool stickle, as the fish steadily went down, till as Will plaintively said, " Zeem's if he'm goin t' Axmouth." When it appeared impossible to stop him by fair means, and the wood was getting thick on the bank, Sam Pitcher, who had run across the field with a two-pronged fork in his hand, was deputed to spear the fish as he passed over the next shallow. Geoff put a heavy strain on the rod, bringing the fish well within Sam's reach; but whether he was nervous, or a sudden twist occurred, or the size, which for the first time revealed to his astonished gaze the lordly proportions of an eighteen pounder, unnerved him, sure it was he missed his stroke, scoring the fish heavily down one side. Any salmon fisher knows the result of a missed gaff stroke on a heavy fish. With a rush that threw Sam head over heels, and pitched the fork yards down stream, the salmon made off, snapping the strong gut as if it had been pack thread. A yell of grief and despair came from Geoff and Will simultaneously, as the rod sprank back with the line floating and useless.

Then it was that Tom Twite covered himself and the whole Twite family with imperishable honour and renown, for snatching up the fork, which floated down the stream, he ran to a shallow, and as the partly exhausted fish rolled and swam past him, pinned it fairly to the bed of the river. "I a got un, I a got un," shouted Tommy, holding on manfully to the fork, de spite the terrific struggles of the smitten fish. In a moment the weight of John Fry was added to the implement, and in a few moments more the prize was lying on the grass.   They could hardly believe in the greatness of their good fortune ; that a salmon, and such a salmon, should be caught in Westcombe water, and that the honour and glory should be fairly attributed to Geoff, with a reflected halo round the tow-like head of Tom Twite, was of all things the most wonderful. It was impossible to say which of the party was the most delighted, but a procession was formed, headed by Geoff and John Fry bearing the fish, flanked by Will with the rod, and Tom Twite with the fork, which nothing would induce him to relinquish.

At the Hall the excitement passed all bounds; Binnell, forgetting his dignity, electrified the Squire and Mrs. Wynheard with the news that "Master Geoff had just caught a zammon zo big as a zow," and the Squire's delighted face formed one of an enthusiastic group, as the whole household gathered round the "fallen monarch of the stream." "He'm five and twenty pound, Id' warnt," said Mrs. Round, surprised out of all politeness, for Mrs. Round did not usually volunteer observations before her betters.

" Bring the scales," said the Squire, and as the fish turned the balance at eighteen pounds, a hum of approval went round. Then it was that Geoff re-counted Tom Twite's share in the capture; a full two inches did that young hero grow as the Squire patted him on the head, and gave him a new half-crown, and to this day John Fry, Sam Pitcher,   and Tom Twite, can jointly and severally tell how Master Geoff caught his " **BIG SALMON.**"

14

FARMER WORSEL MAKES

A SPEECH—

JACK'S HOMECOMING.

Introducing Farmer Worsel & His Workers

CHAPTER XIV.

FARMER WORSEL MAKES A SPEECH.— JACK'S HOME-COMING.

THE home-coming of the young Squire, now Captain Wynheard, was the signal for general rejoicing in and around Westcombe. As the time drew near for the arrival of the ship by which he was expected, the Squire, Mrs. Wynheard, and Geoff, went to Plymouth to meet the invalid, and were delighted to find him recovered from his wound and restored to comparative health. He looked bronzed, soldierly, and, as the Squire said, " a son to be proud of."

In honour of the event, great preparations were made at the Hall, the station, and on the road between the two, and if only Jupiter Pluvius were kind, the reception was certain to be a success. Triumphant arches of evergreen spanned the road, masses of holly, with brilliant paper designs and many other artistic efforts, the spectacular effects of which were so brilliant that the oldest inhabitant failed to remember anything like it, were placed at all available points. There was a gathering of the neighbouring gentry, and the whole of the tenants—in imposing array—headed by a brass band playing martial music, added to these came every other man, woman, and child within a radius of five miles, and the welcome to the recovered hero was likely to be a warm one.

In order that the reception should lose none of its *eclat*, Farmer Worsel, the oldest and most substantial yeoman on the estate, was deputed to present an address and make a speech on the occasion. As the train drew up, to the enlivening strains of "See the Conquering Hero Comes," the party alighted, and the cheers, welcomes, and hand- shakings subsiding, Fanner Worsel came forward to acquit himself like a man. Many a sleepless night and severe heart-searching had his speech caused the honest farmer ; he had consulted the parson, cajoled the clerk, and generally made himself miserable. The Vicar wrote what he termed " a few headings." Friends individually and collectively supplied him with full context. His wife, in the sanctity of their chamber, primed him with points and " memoria technica ;" till, what with mental effort, disquietude, and perspiration, Thomas Worsel lost a full stone in weight.

But, at last, on this—the proudest day of his

life—the oldest tenant made his debut as a public speaker. "Cap'en Winyard," began Worsel, with a face shining like a rising sun from excitement and the sudorific effects of a pint of cider, laced, as th' oldest tenant on Westcombe, "I been deputed to—to——." Here the farmer stuck ; he always had stuck at this point, and his wife allowed that when he got there, "she felt that nervous she went all of a dwam." " To," said Worsel again, and getting desperate, " to drink your very good health," The roar of laughter which followed this commencement put jolly old Worsel at his ease, for subsiding into his natural style, he finished up with, " There, now, I b'aint no hand at a speech, but we'm main glad to see 'ee back", which —with a happy inspiration gathered from a fleeting memory of market dinners— " nobody can deny."

The band ably seconded the suggestion by striking up "For he's a jolly good fellow," and to this spirit-stirring strain the cavalcade set out for the Hall. With Jack at home, the old life returned into its usual groove, and preparations were made for " the great event of the Westcombe year."

The labours of Doggett and Will were now to meet with their full fruition, for the time was drawing near for shooting the great coverts; these woods and spinnies, originally planned and planted by the Squire's grandfather, had been enlarged by the Squire's father, and kept up to a high pitch of perfection, as a sacred duty, by the Squire himself.   They were at once the pride and glory of Westcombe, and the shooting thereof   was held as an annual festival, to be preceded by certain solemn rites and ceremonies.

Firstly came important consultations between the Squire and Doggett, at which Will frequently assisted. *Secondly,* very careful consideration was given to the placing of the guns. *Thirdly,* the beating was arranged—by no means the least important matter. But now, with Jack to assist in the planning and to help in the shooting, the Squire's interest increased tenfold.

The ambition of Doggett and Will was a laudable one, in that they determined there should be a better show of birds every year; rarely had they been disappointed, and this year they were able to announce a brilliant promise; but, as Doggett observed to tlie Squire, " Taint no use, zir, vor we to zhow a lot o' birds ef zo be the genelmen can't zhoot 'em." "Just so," said the Squire regretfully, for a keen sportsman himself and a first-rate shot, nothing annoyed him so much as failure in others ; but, drawing his list out of his pocket, he went carefully over it again. " We want eight guns," said he, " let me see."

" The General, of course." Now General Rolle, besides being a friend and near neighbour, was a fair shot, so could be depended on for his quota. "Major Lee, all right. Mr. Harding?" said the Squire, with a dubious shake of the head. Now Doggett was human, and as Mr. Harding's " tip" was as lavish as his misses were notorious, Doggett interposed hastily with " He'm not to zay a good zhot, aint Mr. Harding, but I've zeed worse, an' we'm put un in a zafe place w'ere a won't zhoot nobody."

" Mr. Blake ? " Here Doggett's eyes glistened: " He'm a nailer, 's Passon Blake, an' 'ceptin' you and Cap'en, zur, there ain't nobody as stops they rocketers like he." " Bird, of Clopton, and the Doctor."

This party was a regular standing dish, the Squire's kindness of heart never allowing him to leave out one. Eight guns were necessary to guard the different points, and for many a year the above gentlemen had met at the covert side, and a very good account they usually gave of the sport provided for them ; but this year more was expected from them, for one or two of the neighbouring estates had run the Westcombe bags hard, and the Squire was very jealous for the honour of his coverts.

He and Jack were exceptional shots, taking their birds just as they came, and rarely failing to stop them fairly hit in front.

The General shot well at first, but, getting excited, would try impossibilities, and missing them invariably, swore hard at his man " Pilcher," who had been his orderly through many a campaign, and was accustomed to it. Major Lee, good all round, made average bags. Harding, one of the best tempered men living, an enthusiastic sportsman and great favourite, could hardly hit a bird except by accident, and not unfrequently peppered a beater.

The Reverend George Blake was, as Doggett described him, " a nailer," a born shot, but, unfortunately, jealous, and had an inordinate opinion of himself and his shooting ; running near but never quite coming up to the Squire and Jack, he made up for Mr. Harding's deficiencies, and never forgot to roast him accordingly. John Bird and our friend the Doctor, who would have been grievously disappointed at being left out, made up the tale ; but this year Geoff was raised to the dignity of a place in the ranks, although the Squire neither considered nor counted him a regular sportsman ; but Doggett had his own views as to Geoff's capacity, and he and Will chuckled over an expected downfall of Parson Blake.

There was one more form to be gone through before this all-important day arrived, and that was a special dinner, where the toast of the evening was the " Forebear who had planted the woods." To this only the intended sportsmen were invited, exception being allowed to the Vicar, who, though no shot, walked with the sportsmen and enjoyed it.

A few days later, on the eve of the shooting, the guests, whose names we have seen, were seated round the Squire's hospitable board, the cloth being removed, for the Squire loved to see the polish of his old mahogany.

Geoff, at a signal from his father, rang the bell ; it was promptly answered by Binnell, bearing a magnum of port of a special vintage. Then did the General's face beam with an anticipatory pleasure, for this was the only occasion, except the christening of Jack and Geoff, when the celebrated Westcombe magnums had been broached. After placing the wine before the Squire in its original bottle, Binnell solemnly presented the cork, which, being duly examined and found sound, was passed round amidst congratulatory murmurs, after the fashion of a sacred calumet.

Then the Squire, gravely passing the bottle, said, "Gentlemen, fill your glasses, and before we drink the toast which is usual on this occasion, you shall hear from the keepers your prospects for to-morrow," Doggett and Will being ushered in, the Squire filled bumpers from the magnum, and presenting one to each, began in an unconcerned tone, as if he knew nothing about it, and as if it had not been the chief topic in his mind for weeks past, " Doggett, the General and these gentlemen want to know what sport they are to expect to-morrow " "Well, zir," said Doggett, " Will 've been very lucky wi' 's young birds this year, we'm turned out nigh upon five hunderd, that's near upon's many's a hatched out, bain't ut, Will ? " "We h'ant lost not to zay zo many," responded Will; "Jarge's zo careful to keep down varmint, an' gapes don't trouble we much." Thus did Doggett and Will always praise one another, there being an entire absence of rivalry between the two ; and the enthusiasm of the party being kindled to a high pitch by this satisfactory report, the Squire proposed the toast of the evening, and they drank with due solemnity to the ancestor to whose forethought they were indebted for their prospective pleasure.

Feeding Pheasant Chicks

Pheasants Being Reared

OLD STYLE PHEASANT SHOOTING

15

SHOOTING THE GREAT

COVERTS

At the Ready

CHAPTER XV.

SHOOTING THE GREAT COVERTS

TEN o'clock on a beautiful crisp morning in November found the party who had dined together the previous evening ready for the work of the day. There was no doubt they meant to enjoy themselves, and not only they, but a contingent from the village of all the male population capable of bearing sticks.

As shooting the great coverts was for Westcombe a yearly festival, there were grouped together near the covert side the tenants and their sons, foremost amongst whom shone Old Worsel, with a face of roseate hue and broad enjoyment; there were the labourers ; there, too, in the everlasting velveteens, and gaiters, were keepers from neighbouring estates, who had come partly to help and partly to criticise ; in the background, forming no inconsiderable addition to the day's delight, were well-filled baskets, stone bottles and firkins ; there, too, was Doggett, in great though suppressed excitement, for he well knew the onerous nature of the task before him in controlling this willing but erratic crowd—It was morally certain that before the day was over one or two would receive a dose of No. 4 shot, or what the Doctor, last season, with very grim jocularity termed an "Emplastrum Plumbi;" and it was enough to drive a scientific keeper to distraction to attempt to keep a line that would wave, bend, and break, however much you objurgated it; so he welcomed the chance of pointing his moral by recalling the howls of Sam Vittles, when Mr. Harding last year put a charge of shot into the rear of that astonished beater, who would persistently keep sixty yards in advance of the rest of the line. Our old friend, Will, was hobbling about radiant with pride and expectation, for on this day he occupied the coveted post of loader to the Squire. Half the party were two-gun men : the Squire, Jack, the General, Major Lee shooting with pairs ; but Parson Blake, Geoff, Mr. Harding and the Doctor, were content to use one gun each.

As the sportsmen reached the covert side, a welcoming murmur arose, and Old Worsel, shaking hands heartily with Jack, congratulated him on his recovered looks, with " Proud to zee 'e, Cap'en ; you'm do zeem a bit pearter like." There was no difficulty or hurry in placing the guns, for all arrangements had been perfected the day before, and Doggett showed the point where each was to stand.

The Squire insisted on all the party being fairly placed, he taking one flank, and Jack the other, whilst Parson Blake and Major Lee walked with the beaters. We have mentioned the coverts as great woods, but they were really grown in blocks, with drives between sufficiently wide to separate and form them into a chain

The Shoot Was Now In Progress

of divided spinnies. Nothing could be more advantageous for keen sportsmen, as the birds came over the tree tops fast and high.

At a signal from Doggett, the line of beaters advanced, making far more noise than is accordant with the advanced views of now-a-day's practice ; but those beaters were out for enjoyment, a real holiday, and did not trouble them-selves with the refinements of sport.

Observations

At the beginning of a drive it is interesting to the close observer to note the habits of the animals and the flight and ways of the different birds. The first to scurry off is the sparrow hawk or kestrel, if one has survived the watchful eye of the keeper; experience in their case is an excellent teacher, for they go judgematically, without appearance of undue hurry, but with an astonishingly keen eye for the disposition of the guns, and a look which seems to say—" Never mind—never mind me. I'll call again another day."

Then comes the clip-clap, clip-clap of the wood pigeons, as they dash out, and topping the trees, wing away into space. You may next hear the jays' chatter, chatter, chatter, but very soon their conversational powers are subdued, as they eagerly watch for a chance to slip from tree to tree to the next covert.

As the beaters advance, you catch the alarm note of a cock black-bird or two, and soon the advanced guard of a band of linnets and finches comes flying over, shortly followed by the main body ; then a keen eye will note a hare, perhaps two, jogging quietly, but with obvious intention, to a quiet corner, where puss hopes to slip out unobserved; pausing and listening with wonderful keenness, she makes her point, just thirty yards are traversed, and then heels over head rolls a mass of fur, and lies motionless on the dewy grass. Now is it that that wily biped, the old cock pheasant, who has survived previous shoots, thinks it time to skedaddle and he slinks along close to the wall, railing, or maybe down a ditch, hoping to escape ; it takes a great deal to spring him into the air, until he thinks he is safe, when he sails away with the most sarcastic of chuckles. Rabbits are now pattering about, but as a rule they lie close, and require to be poked out, when they make for the nearest burrow at a tremendous pace. "How is it," says the disgusted owner to the underkeeper, who is loading for him, "that there are so few birds in this covert?"

The question is answered at once by a view halloo, and amidst a storm of yells, running easily but with every sense on the alert, comes an old dog fox, who has been playing high jinks with the pheasants, if we may judge by the gloss and condition of his fur.

We have strayed from our covert shooting for a few moments to lift a veil, and to see as yet no pheasants have got up. As the line progresses, there arise shouts of "Mark over—over—mark over !" and a lordly cock pheasant, rejoicing in his strength, rises high above the trees, heading straight for the Captain. A slight throw back of the gun as the bird gets nearly vertical—a puff of smoke—a stagger in the steady flight—and an inert mass of golden plumage falls with a thud behind that fortunate officer, whilst a tuft or two of feathers float softly away. More yells and shouts, as bird after bird rises—three and four in the air together; for a minute the shooting gets wild, for they are beating too quickly, but a running- fire of expletives, passed down the line from Doggett, arrests the too willing hands, and the shooting steadies.

They are now three quarters through the first wood ; the Squire has never shot better, and old Will keeps up a running comment as bird after bird drops: "You'm in beautiful form, zir, zurely;" "Lank a massy, but that were a gran' zhot," as a fast rocketer far off fell like a stone, and the Squire is pleased.

CHINESE PHEASANT (*Phasianus torquatus*).

At First the Pheasants were Slow to Rise

Jack and the others have done their duty, too; Geoff has toppled some of the rocketers over in a way that made the Doctor laughingly congratulate himself on not being a pheasant, and even the General has so far been urbane and confiding to Pitcher, who hands him his second gun. As the line draws on, the birds rise rapidly ; then it is that steadiness is required, both in loading and shooting. The General gets excited, fires wildly, and begins to lose control.

Pilcher, although used to it, also loses his presence of mind, and in handing a gun to the choleric officer, discharges one barrel within an ace of the General's legs, and shaves the retriever, who, unused to such treatment, forms a duet with his exasperated master.

All this time the pheasants are streaming over, and the first drive is finished, to the General's chagrin, without his landing a bird in the final flurry,

Great satisfaction was expressed by all concerned; even the General had cooled, and now they attack the second and most difficult wood of the day : here it is that really artistic shooting is required ; the stations are in a hollow. the birds fly high to cross to the next covert. In this wood it was the Squire's privilege to take one of the difficult places, Jack the other, and Parson Blake, for the first time, took the third ;

SPARROWHAWK

Sparrow Hawks
One flew away from the scene of the Shoot.

none of the others could kill a bird, and they knew it, so the arrangement was satisfactory to all concerned, more   especially as other points required stopping, and birds were plentiful.

But Doggett and Will had their doubts about even Parson Blake's capacity for so difficult a performance, and casually suggested that Geoff might stand behind the Parson and take, "what he chose to let go". The Parson had no objection, as Geoff was quite welcome to anything that passed him.

The covert was long and narrow, but, with the exception of the Holmwood, held more birds than any other. The guns placed, the last commands uttered, and the beat commenced. "Mark over" was shouted almost immediately, as a grand long-tailed fellow went streaming towards the hollow—Parson Blake's bird ! The Parson, just a trifle nervous, for many critical eyes were watching him, forgot to allow for the height and tremendous pace, and shot behind ; slewing round, he tried the other barrel, and missed again. It was now Geoff s turn, when, to the disgust of the older sportsman, the lad nicked his bird, bringing him down dead as a door-nail. " Well done, Master Geoff" shouted Will, almost beside himself at his favourite's success ; but that was not all, for another cock pheasant makes tracks in the line of the first, only to fall to Geoff s second barrel, the Parson objurgating his ill-luck at having to load both ; and now an astonishing tiling happened : Parson Blakelost his nerve, and went off his shooting altogether; usually a capital shot, he was almost crying as bird after bird sailed harmlessly over, the most part to fall to the gun of Geoff, until eighteen birds were killed by the two, of which one cock and two hens represented the Parson's total.

Will was in his element, and loaded with a skill and rapidity that kept the Squire always ready ; of course he missed a few—everyone does—but they were very few, and, as is often the case, not the most difficult shots.

When the drive was over, twenty-seven birds had fallen to the Squire, twenty to Jack, fifteen to Geoff, and three to the disgusted Parson ; and Will, recounting the incident, chuckled with Doggett as to the way in which "Master Geoff" had " wiped Parson Blake's eye."

The other gentlemen had done fairly well, and the bag was rising fast. As the day was advancing, lunch was served, and a merry, happy party sat down.

" Ah, Worsel! this is better than gruel! " shouted the Doc with his mouth glued to the special special firkin. " Ay, or doctors' stuff either," said Worsel, giv-

.

ing as good as he got.

"What's the joke?" said the General, who loved a story   " Well" said the Doctor, Old Worsel there, who weighs nineteen stone if he's a pound, got into trouble last summer haymaking, for nothing would satisfy him but getting between the ricks and the cart's tail ; the rick, of course, would not move, and the cart felt much the same way, so Worsel, after being squeezed black in the face, was picked up nearly dead, and I was sent for.

I reached the house in half-an-hour, and found him in bed, with the sweat pouring off him, and if you'll believe me," said the Doctor solemnly, " *a wash-hand-basin of gruel* nearly emptied before him."

I shall never forget the agonised expression of his face, as he shovelled another spoonful in, at the urgent entreaty of his wife and daughter. " Oh, Doctor I" they both said, " we'm zo glad you be com'd, for vather zays"—pointing to the basin— "he won't take another, an they 've stove 'es ribs right in wi' th' cart, an we'm blowin em out beautiful."   The roars of laughter which followed this tale were repeated again and again, as the probable appearance of Old Worsel during his gruelling was pictured on the minds of the audience.

Just then the General's retriever made his wants known by a raid on his master's plate, and that reminded the General how nearly he had lost his favourite dog, and he told of Pilcher's delinquencies with a face so serious as to provoke fresh merriment.

Now Pilcher was the General's special facto-tum, and, as we have before stated, had been his orderly, but being a thoroughbred cockney, and as innocent of rural pursuits as a new-born babe, had, by a special freak of fortune, been selected by the gallant, though choloeric old officer to superintend his Game preserves.

Dire and awful was the grief to which Pilcher occasionally came, but somehow the General stuck to him with a tenacity worthy of a better object. The keepers, one and all, would snigger at Pilcher, for he never had the wit to keep quiet, but exposed himself with a reck-lessness born of supreme ignorance. Early in the season Pilcher had very nearly gone beyond the length of his tether with his master.

It happened in the second week in September that the Squire invited one or two guns for partridge shooting ; towards the close of the day some scattered birds rose from a field of standing beans ; after three or four had risen, a young and confiding hen pheasant followed rather to the right of the General, who rewarded her confidence by promptly potting her. In a moment the General was aware of the enormity of his offence !! !

Partridges

After Philip Rickman

" The Squire invited one or two guns
for partridge shooting".

to kill a young hen pheasant on a friend's ground !!! early in September !!! Cold sweat poured down the unhappy officer's back, and he could only hope no one had seen her fall ; not so Pilcher, who, walking behind his master, rejoiced in the goodly sight of what he took for an unusually plump partridge, and shouted to the guilt-stricken General, "A bird down here, sir." "Come on," said the General decisively. " There's a bird here, I seen it fall." persisted Pilcher. "Come on, I tell you," repeated the disgusted officer. "It's in that corner, sir; I'm sure it's dead," reiterated Pilcher. " Come on, you —— fool," roared the wrath-stricken General, "or I'll——." What the General would have done no one knew, but very reluctantly Pilcher came away.

At the end of the day's sport the game was counted. " Twenty-four and a half brace," announced the Squire ; "just forty-nine birds." At that moment Pilcher advanced, and, making a military salute, presented the General's contribution—the dishevelled little pheasant poult—with "fifty, if you please, sir, and the finest partridge in the lot." It is well to draw a veil over the torrents of wrath that poured from the General, but the roars of laughter from the rest were so loud and long that they shook even Pilcher's complacency.

After lunch the rest of the woods and spinnies were beaten, but I am not going- to try my reader's patience with vain repetitions ;   it is sufficient to say that Parson Blake rehabilitated himself in his own opinion and that of the rest.

In a moment the General was aware of the enormity of his offence !! ! to kill a young hen pheasant on a friend's ground !!! early in September !!! Cold sweat poured down the unhappy officer's back, and he could only hope no one had seen her fall ; not so Pilcher, who, walking behind his master, rejoiced in the goodly sight of what he took for an unusually plump partridge, and shouted to the guilt-stricken General, "A bird down here, sir." "Come on," said the General decisively. " There's a bird here, I seen it fall." persisted Pilcher. "Come on, I tell you," repeated the disgusted officer. "It's in that corner, sir; I'm sure it's dead," reiterated Pilcher. " Come on, you —— fool," roared the wrath-stricken General, "or I'll——." What the General would have done no one knew, but very reluctantly Pilcher came away.

At the end of the day's sport the game was counted. " Twenty-four and a half brace," announced the Squire ; "just forty-nine birds." At that moment Pilcher advanced, and, making a military salute, presented the General's contribution—the dishevelled little pheasant poult—with "fifty, if you please, sir, and the finest partridge in the lot." It is well to draw a veil over the torrents of wrath that poured from the General, but the roars of laughter from the rest were long and loud.

I am not going- to try my reader's patience with vain repetitions ; it is sufficient to say that Parson Blake rehabilitated himself in his own opinion and that of the rest of the party, by bringing down his birds as of old;that the dear old Squire's hand in no way forgot its cunning, nor for the matter of that did Mr. Harding's, for he perforated the smallclothes of Bill Sloecomb with no less than sixteen pellets, causing thereby much physical anguish to that gentle spirit; but a golden salve, of which a not inconsiderable portion melted at the Blue Cow, soothed his woes and mended the aforesaid small-clothes.

Great was the glory, and radiant became the faces of Doggett and Will as the bag totalled by far the largest ever killed over Westcornbe. Peace and plenty reigned far and near, for the Squire was no niggard, and every farmer had a brace of pheasants, and every villager a couple of rabbits.

The Squire held, and I agree with him, that the right way to enjoy sport is to give the farmer and the labourer an interest in the result, and by this means you will double your pleasure and your bags.

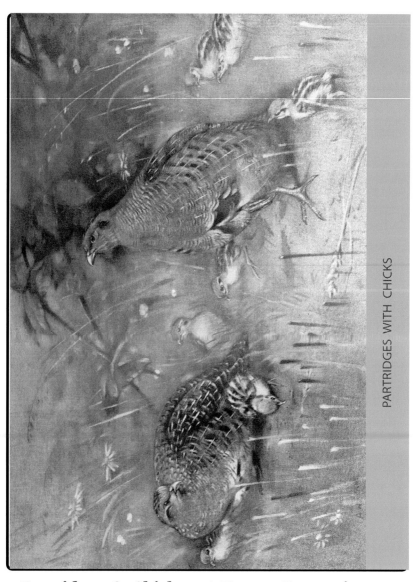

Partridges & Chicks -- A Future Generation

The dear old Squire's hand in no way forgot its cunning, nor for the matter of that did Mr. Harding's, for he perforated the small-clothes of Bill Sloecomb with no less than sixteen pellets, causing thereby much physical anguish to that gentle spirit ; but a golden salve, of which a not inconsiderable portion melted at the Blue Cow, soothed his woes and mended the aforesaid small-clothes.

Great was the glory, and radiant became the faces of Doggett and Will as the bag totalled by far the largest ever killed over Westcombe. Peace and plenty reigned far and near, for the Squire was no niggard, and every farmer had a brace of pheasants, and every villager a couple of rabbits. The Squire held, and I agree with him, that the right way to enjoy sport is to give the farmer and the labourer an interest in the result, and by this means you will double your pleasure and your bags.

     *   *   *   *   *   *   *

Thirty years have passed away—thirty golden summers come and silver winters gone since first we wandered midst the pleasant woods of Westcombe, and now is winter once again upon us, enwrapping all the silent landscape with a vast winding sheet. Few have been the changes that have passed over our friends.

The old Squire and his wife , forty years have dwelt together in the home they love so well. Jack, now Colonel Wynheard, lives at Westcombe the pleasant life of a country gentleman. Geoff, a rising young barrister, visits the Hall as often as he can, whilst the old Vicar, now frail and white-headed, but bright and cheerful as of yore, is ready to sing his *"nunc dimittis."*

Time, too, has dealt gently with George and Will ; like David and Jonathan, their single-hearted affection has become a by-word, and together the two old men are moving down the hill of that life they have done so much to ennoble.

The snow had been falling heavily all day, but towards the afternoon there was a lull; still, the clouds looked grey and heavy, and occasional flakes gave further promise. Many a time had the old Squire looked longingly out of the window, for Geoff was expected, and the night was drawing on. At last the lamps shone in the distance, and a few minutes later the brothers were in the Hall. "A bad night, sir, and worse to follow," said the Colonel, stamping the snow off his feet. " So it is, so it is," assented the Squire, " but we'll keep it out." Happy was the Squire in both his sons; neither had given him appreciable anxiety; the Colonel, we know, was all that a man should, be, and he had exercised a wonderful influence over his brother— an influence that tided Geoff over the many sloughs of a young barrister's life. Geoff had had his fling, and spent a good deal of money whilst at college and on circuit, but the Colonel helped him, and the Squire paid the bills with a grumble, and Geoff was now settling down into a very industrious young fellow, with an occasional brief.

The party had just finished dinner, and were drawing near the fire, when Binnell, the old butler, entered hurriedly to say that Sally Twite (one of the olive branches of Tom Twite, of salmon fame) had come from the keeper's lodge, and was crying because Doggett had not returned from his rounds, and Will had gone out to find him.

"Bless my heart!" said the startled Squire, " bring her in." Sally Twite's tale, simply told, was that George Doggett had gone out after dinner to visit some traps near the river, and had not returned—as the evening drew on Will had become restless and anxious, and suddenly starting up would go out, declaring he heard Doggett calling him ; but, said Sally, " There wor'nt no one calling, and if there wor, Will's as deaf as deaf, an' coulden hear em, an' I waited an' waited till I wer that vrightened I com'd here."

With a glance at the Squire, the two brothers rose together. "Binnell," said the Squire, "get all the men and lanthorns, and rouse the village. Jack ! you take one party andgo by the meadows, and Geoff will go through the woods. Take your flasks, but I feel very anxious." In a surprisingly short time two bands of ready helpers set out on their search ; the night was dark and the snow drifting, but little cared they for that—whilst from every house in the village glimmered reassuring lights ; minute after minute crept on—-an hour passed—still no sign of the missing men.

They had reached the river, near the spot where Will was so nearly drowned, when a shout from one of the searchers brought the party together. The buzz of voices suddenly hushed as a terrible presentiment forced itself upon them : there, in a little hollow, lay all that was left of George Doggett and Will Murrill—side by side lay the old men -- Will's arm thrown lovingly round Doggett's neck, and his head resting on Doggett's shoulder. Accustomed as he was to death on the battlefield, the Colonel's voice was very husky, as he took a hand of each and said, " My dear old friends." Sob upon sob burst from the circle of grief stricken searchers as they fully realised the calamity.

Loving hands lifted George and Will from their resting place, and laid them reverently on extemporised stretcher; and then a sad procession moved homewards. It wa evident that Doggett had died early in the day—heart disease the Doctor called it. How then did Will find him?

Did the wonderful instinct of love and affection prove a: unerring guide ? for an- old, feeble, and crippled man could scarcely have searched; yet

THE EPITAPH.

Here rests his head upon the lap of Earth
    A youth to Fortune and to Fame unknown;
Fair Science frown'd not on his humble birth,
    And Melancholy mark'd him for her own.

Thomas Gray
ELEGY

Murrill must have gone straigh to the spot, found his friend, and then ! his loving heart had broken. Sad, indeed, was the home coming; door after door poured forth its sobbing women and grief stricken men, and midst a crowd of sympathisers, the remains of George Doggett and Will Murrill were carried home.

If the grief of one was deeper than that of other though less demonstrative, it was that of Phoebe Trip, who as Phoebe Fitton thirty years before had discarded Doggett.

Phoebe it was, now a grey-haired woman, who insisted on performing the last sad offices for the two men, before they were taken to their resting place.

Then, the old Vicar, a voice tremulous with emotion, gave "dust to dust," while the Snow Queen very softly and tenderly scattered the lovely though chilling wreaths, and even to this day you will hear from the lips of the Westcombe villagers the sad story of the tragedy, and how George and Will, *"beautiful and pleasant in their lives, were not divided"*.

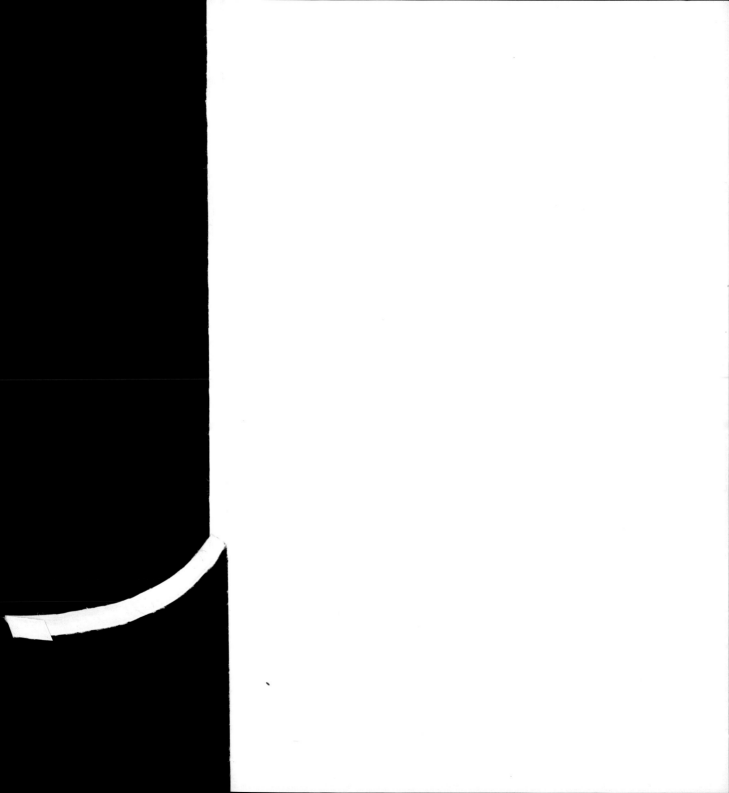